On the Game

On the Game

Monique Polak

James Lorimer & Company Ltd., Publishers
Toronto

FIC
POL

© 2005 Monique Polak

James Lorimer & Company Ltd. acknowledges the support of the Ontario Arts Council. We acknowledge the support of the Government of Canada through the Book Publishing Industry Development Program (BPIDP) for our publishing activities. We acknowledge the support of the Canada Council for the Arts for our publishing program. We acknowledge the support of the Government of Ontario through the Ontario Media Development Corporation's Ontario Book Initiative.

The Canada Council | Le Conseil des Arts
for the Arts | du Canada

ONTARIO ARTS COUNCIL
CONSEIL DES ARTS DE L'ONTARIO

Cover design: Clarke MacDonald

Canada Cataloguing in Publication Data

Polak, Monique
    On the game / Monique Polak.

(SideStreets)
ISBN 10 1-55028-876-8 (pbk.)
ISBN 13 978-1-55028-876-6 (pbk.)
ISBN 10 1-55028-877-6 (bound)
ISBN 13 978-1-55028-877-3 (bound)

I. Title.

PS8631.O43O5 2005   jC813'.6   C2005-900263-8

James Lorimer & Company Ltd., Publishers
317 Adelaide St West, Suite 1002
Toronto, Ontario
M5V 1P9
www.lorimer.ca
Printed and bound in Canada

Distributed in the United States by:
Orca Book Publishers,
P.O. Box 468
Custer, WA USA
98240-0468

For Pa,
who taught us that
it's okay to make mistakes.

Acknowledgments

Special thanks to James Lorimer, who believed this story needed to be told. Thanks, also, to the many people who shared their expertise about the world of "the game": Michel Dorais, professor of social work at Université Laval and expert witness at the trials of several Quebec City pimps involved in juvenile prostitution; police officer T.M.; Phebeth Dawkins and Peter Desmier, youth workers at Batshaw Youth and Family Centre in Montreal; Peter's cigar bar cronies; and the sex workers who agreed to talk with me on the condition their names not be mentioned.

Thanks as well to Hadley Dyer, editor extraordinaire, and to the team at James Lorimer; to my father, Judge Maximilien Polak, for sharing his insights into the criminal justice system; to both him and my mother, Celine Polak, for reading the first draft of this project; to my students, for filling me in on the party scene; to Jessica Haberman, for teaching me dance moves; to Rhea Westover and Deena Sacks, for reading the first draft; to Viva Singer, for standing by me and for talking me through the story, chapter by chapter; to my daughter, Alicia Melamed, for always answering the question, "How does this sound?"; to my writing friends, Rina Singh, Claire Holden Rothman and Elaine Kalman Naves, for their encouragement and fine example. Finally, extra special thanks to my kind and clever husband, Michael Shenker, whose love and encouragement make all my writing possible.

Chapter 1

Yolande twisted her wrist to show off the bracelet. "It's a Tiffany," she said, pointing her other hand to the tiny block letters on the heart dangling from the silver links: TIFFANY & CO. "*He* gave it to me," Yolande added breathlessly.

"He *did?*" Gabrielle said, as Yolande unlatched the bracelet and placed it on her friend's wrist. "Wow."

"These too," Yolande said, reaching under her bed and pulling out a shoebox. She lifted a pair of black patent-leather stilettos from a bed of tissue paper.

For a second, Gabrielle held her breath. "They're so-o-o sexy," she said at last. "What are you going to wear them with?"

"My jean miniskirt. I was wearing it the night we met. He said he was picturing me in the skirt when he saw the shoes. He says he thinks about me all the time."

"He does?"

The two girls were sitting cross-legged on the carpet in Yolande's bedroom. A photograph of her dad smiled out at them from a silver frame on her bureau. Not so long ago, she and Gabrielle had played Snakes and Ladders and Barbies on this same pale-pink carpet. Sometimes, those Barbie games had lasted all afternoon. They'd trade Barbie clothes, march their Barbies across the room, and pretend their Barbies had fallen in love.

Now Yolande was in love. And she had a bracelet and shoes to prove it.

"You'll meet someone, too. I know you will," Yolande said as she watched Gabrielle remove the bracelet from her wrist. "I just hope he'll be as great as Etienne."

Gabrielle cupped the bracelet in her hand. "Remember what Madame Leroux told us about jewelry when we were studying ancient Egypt?"

Yolande tilted her head back so her pale-blonde hair fell halfway down her back, and laughed. It was her trademark laugh: deep and throaty. "That was the only interesting thing we learned all year. 'One of the earliest forms of jewelry were the slave rings masters made their slaves wear,'" she said in a nasal voice meant to be an imitation of Madame Leroux. "Well, I'll tell you something," and here she rolled her eyes for dramatic effect, "If Etienne wanted me to be his slave, I'd say yes."

"Yo-yo!" Gabrielle sounded stern. "We've been

10

friends since kindergarten, but I still can't always tell when you're joking. That was a joke, right?"

"Of course it was," Yolande said, cracking up.

"So when do I get to meet him?" Gabrielle looked into Yolande's eyes, which were the same greyish blue as the sky before a summer storm.

Yolande hesitated. "Soon, I guess. Maybe even this weekend. It all depends on his schedule."

The girls heard the shuffle of footsteps on the stairway leading to Yolande's bedroom. Yolande slid the shoebox under the bed. "Quick!" she whispered. "Hide the bracelet!"

Gabrielle stashed the bracelet under the bed, then smoothed the eyelet bed skirt. She reached for the *Cosmopolitan* magazine lying open on the floor. "So Yo-yo, what do you think of this top?" she asked in a loud voice.

"Hmm …" Yolande pretended to be checking out a T-shirt, though the page was open to a perfume ad of a half-naked blonde. "A little too low-cut," she said, winking at Gabrielle.

The girls were not surprised to hear the rat-a-tat-tat of Yolande's mother knocking at the door. Sheila Owen used the inside of her hand to tap, so her wedding band made contact with the wood. Though her husband had been dead for seven years, she still wore the ring.

"Girls," she said, beaming down at them, "I'm headed out. There's a platter on the kitchen table with lettuce, tomatoes, carrot sticks, and sliced cheese." She'd been on a mission all summer to get Yolande to eat more vegetables. "What are your plans?"

"We're going to read fashion magazines," Gabrielle said.

But, as usual, Yolande had other, more exciting plans. "No, we're going out too," she announced, getting up from the floor, her legs as long and lanky as a colt's. "Don't worry, Mom. We'll finish all our veggies," she said in her dutiful daughter voice.

"Where are you off to?" Mrs. Owen asked.

"No place special." Yolande met her mother's gaze. "The schoolyard, Girouard Park, maybe Monkland."

Monkland was the main thoroughfare in Notre-Dame de-Grâce, the Montreal neighbourhood where they lived. When the girls were little, Monkland had been a sleepy street with little more than a couple of butcher shops, a tavern, and a bank. But in the last five years, the street had grown up, too.

A Starbucks and a Second Cup vied for customers, and there were so many restaurants and bars it was hard to find parking. The locals came mostly on foot so that, in summer, the street became a kind of boardwalk. All that was missing was a beach and souvenir stands.

"You know my rule: Home before dark," Mrs. Owen said, wagging her finger in the air. Then she smiled at Yolande. "Aren't you a lucky girl to have a mom who's so devoted to you?"

"Aren't I?" Yolande forced a smile.

Mrs. Owen leaned down to peck Yolande on the cheek.

Yolande rolled her eyes.

"How are things at your house, Gabs?" Mrs. Owen asked.

"Oh, you know, same as always. It's Dad's week to stay with us. Which means pizza and TSN."

"Sounds like fun," said Mrs. Owen, and she shut the bedroom door. Gabrielle's parents were divorced, but in an attempt not to disrupt their daughters' lives, they took turns sharing the family home.

"Is she going to meditate?" Gabrielle asked after they heard the front door close.

"It's all she ever does — besides go to the office and the grocery store. Now how pathetic is that?" Yolande had changed from shorts into her miniskirt and was slipping her feet into the stilettos. The heels were three inches high, making her legs look even longer. "What do you think, Gabs?" she asked, laughing as she spun around and managed, somehow, not to lose her balance.

"You remind me of the ballerina inside that jewelry box I gave you in grade two. Only you look way hotter. Hey, how did he know your shoe size, anyway?"

"I was wondering that, too. So I asked him," Yolande said. "Know what he said? That he's the kind of guy who pays attention to detail. Now how cool is that?"

"Cool. Definitely."

"You can't be seen in public in those cut-offs, Gabs. Here, try this!" Yolande reached into her closet and handed Gabrielle a skimpy, pink tank-top dress.

"Hey, isn't this like your best dress?"

"Hey, aren't you like my best friend?"

"I don't think it's me," Gabrielle said, holding the dress up over her rumpled white T-shirt.

"You don't know if it's you 'til you try it on."

Yolande whistled when Gabrielle modelled the dress. The fabric clung to her body. Shorter and less curvaceous than her friend, Gabrielle had a fit, athletic build. The pink set off her dark curls, which fell to her shoulders. "I don't know," Gabrielle said, blushing when she saw herself in the mirror.

"It looks great! C'mon, party girl, time for makeup!" Yolande led Gabrielle to her bureau, which was covered with makeup containers and bottles of body spray.

"Let's get something to eat," Yolande said when they'd finished applying eyeliner, sparkly eyeshadow, and lip gloss.

In the kitchen, Yolande emptied the plate of veggies into a plastic bag. "If I bury this at the bottom of the trash can," she said, opening the cupboard under the sink where they stored garbage, "she'll never know."

"Yo-yo," Gabrielle said, shaking her head, "shouldn't we at least eat some?"

Yolande reached into the bag and pulled out a handful of carrot sticks, all carefully scraped clean. She put one between her lips and pretended to puff on it. She passed the rest to Gabrielle. "Here," she said, "your daily dose of beta carotene." Then she took four slices of multi-grain bread from a bag in the fridge. "D'ya want mayo or mustard on your cheese sandwich?"

"Mayo, please. Yo-yo, you'd better use a plate. Your mom hates crumbs."

"With all her meditating, you figure she'd get over crap like that. Let's eat on the way."

"Where're we going anyhow?"

"You'll see once we get there."

"Didn't your mom say she wants you home before dark?"

"Relax, Gabs, we're fifteen, not five. Besides, it's almost July. It doesn't get dark till nine-thirty. Think of all the trouble we can get into before then."

Chapter 2

"So *did* you?"

Yolande crossed her legs. The stilettos showed off her calves, which were tanned and shapely. She and Gabrielle were sitting on a wrought-iron bench at the edge of the schoolyard. Classes at Sacred Angels Academy, the school the girls had gone to since grade 1, had been over for two weeks, but this bench, nestled beneath a huge red maple, was still one of their favourite spots.

Yolande kicked at the sandwich bag she'd let fall to the ground. Her toenails were painted a fiery red.

Gabrielle bent down to pick up the bag before it flew off into the warm evening air. Folding it into a square, she tucked it into the outside pocket of her purse. "I guess that means you did. Right?"

Yolande looked up into Gabrielle's eyes. "Okay, right. We did. And it was amazing. Etienne Garon's amazing. He makes me feel amazing."

"Well, that's — that's amazing. But —"
Gabrielle hesitated for a moment — "did it hurt?"

"Nah. Well, maybe a little — at first. But not
after that. No, like I told you, it was amazing."

"Where'd you do it?" Gabrielle asked, her
questions coming more easily now. She stooped
down to pluck a long blade of grass and slid it
between her lips.

"His apartment."

"He has an apartment?" Gabrielle nearly
choked on the grass.

"Uh-huh. Downtown. On St-Denis street."

"I figured he lived with his family."

"He doesn't."

"Yo-yo, how old is this guy?"

Yolande giggled. "Now don't go getting all
judgmental on me, Gabs. I didn't get around to
telling you this yet, but Etienne's a little older."

"How old?" Gabrielle could be very persistent.

"Twenty-one," Yolande announced, watching
Gabrielle's face as if she were daring her to object.

"That means he's six years older than us,"
Gabrielle said, trying to keep her voice even.

"I knew all that math homework would pay off
some day, Gabs. Take fifteen away from twenty-
one and you have six. So yes, Etienne is six years
older than us," Yolande said, rolling her eyes.
"You didn't expect me to fall in love with some
pimply guy from grade ten, did you? By the way,"
she added, lowering her voice, "there's something
else I haven't told you about him."

17

"What's that?"

"He's Haitian."

Gabrielle whistled. "You're having sex with a guy who's twenty-one and black? What'll your mom say?"

"Nothing — since I'm not planning to tell her. I figure, why disturb all that Zen peace she works so hard for?" Yolande brought her palms together, raising them to her heart in prayer position. Then she bowed her head and laughed.

"How do you know he's not just using you?" Gabrielle asked in a quiet voice. "He isn't. I just know," Yolande said, flicking away a ladybug that had landed on her elbow.

"Did you use a condom?"

"What do you think I am — stupid? Of course we did. In fact, now that I've discovered sex, I keep protection with me at all times. Just in case." Yolande picked up her crocheted pink purse from the bench. "See?" she said, unzipping it so Gabrielle could look inside.

Yolande burst into laughter as Gabrielle peered inside the bag. "I — I — can't believe you fell for that!" Yolande managed to say between spurts of laughter.

"What are these for?" Gabrielle asked, taking a pair of metal handcuffs from Yolande's purse.

Yolande had forgotten about the handcuffs. "They're for — you know …"

"Don't tell me they're Tiffany too," Gabrielle said, which made them both laugh so hard they nearly toppled off the bench.

"I've got something else in here," Yolande said, grabbing her purse from Gabrielle's lap. Yolande reached inside and pulled out a spray can. She shook the can up and down as she eyed the sign near the gate: *Sacred Angels Academy.*

"You can get arrested for that, you know."

Either Yolande didn't know or she didn't care. She ran toward the sign, the spray can poised in one hand, ready for action.

The paint was the same shade of red as Yolande's toenails. Splattered on the white sign, it looked like blood. *"ANGELS ARE"* Yolande wrote in big, bold letters that seemed to lean in on each other.

Then she passed the can to Gabrielle who had followed Yolande to the gate. "You finish!"

"Are you nuts?" Gabrielle said, pushing away the can.

"Try it! Just try it!" Yolande insisted, unprying Gabrielle's fingers and forcing her to take the can. "Just see what it feels like," she said, pressing Gabrielle's thumb down on the trigger.

Gabrielle giggled as a thick line of red paint came spurting from the can, landing in a gooey puddle at her feet. "Okay. I tried it."

"No, you didn't. Go on. Finish it up," said Yolande, pointing at the sentence she'd started.

It didn't take long for Gabrielle to finish Yolande's sentence. When she was done, Gabrielle stepped away from the sign to survey her work.

Directly underneath the words *Sacred Angels Academy* was another sentence: *ANGELS ARE DEAD*.

Chapter 3

"We'll work on it some more tomorrow. I promise."

Aggie moaned. "You're always sleeping over at Yo-yo's," she said to her sister, who was putting the cap on a bottle of white glue. "Now I'm stuck watching golf with Dad."

"You know you *could* work on the collage without us," Yolande suggested.

Aggie's mouth dropped into a pout.

The three girls were in Gabrielle and Aggie's den, working on a collage of old family photos and postcards of places the sisters had travelled to. New York City, Banff, and two Christmases ago — before their parents had separated — Fort Lauderdale.

"For the record," Yolande said, "she doesn't always sleep over at my house."

"It feels like she does," Aggie said.

Yolande couldn't argue with that.

Aggie — her name was short for Agathe — had

Gabrielle's curls, only they were blonde and softer looking. Even at twelve, with her breasts beginning to bud and her hips to widen, Aggie still had a baby-faced innocence about her.

As Gabrielle got up from the sofa, she pulled one of Aggie's blonde ringlets and let it spring back into place. "Good luck with the golf."

* * *

"I rented three DVDs. *Clueless*, *The Craft*, and *Save the Last Dance*." Yolande rattled off the names of the movies in a loud voice as she and Gabrielle walked into the house. Then she winked at Gabrielle.

"Hi, girls," Yolande's mom called from the kitchen. "What do you two say to an early dinner? I was thinking of bean burgers and sa—"

"—lad," Yolande said. It was easy to finish her mom's sentences. "Sounds good, Mom. That'll give Gabs and me time for our movie marathon."

"I'm so pleased you two are staying home tonight," Mrs. Owen said, humming to herself as she stirred the pot of black beans on the stove. "I once read how the sleep you get before midnight counts for double. Besides, I have *satsang* first thing tomorrow, so I need to be in bed early myself. Any chance you girls want to come along in the morning?"

"What is *satsang*?" Gabrielle asked as she followed Yolande into the kitchen. A photo of a smiling guru with a white beard that grew almost down to his knees was displayed on the refrigerator door.

"Literally, it's Sanskrit for 'company of the saints,'" Mrs. Owen answered. "At our Sunday morning *satsangs*, we chant and meditate. Then there's a spiritual lesson and Indian tea."

"I don't know why they call it tea. It's more like Indian milk — with a little tea in it," Yolande said. "We'd love to come, Mom, honestly we would — but maybe next time."

"Okay then," Mrs. Owen said, "maybe next time."

After dinner and more talk of Mrs. Owen's meditation practices, Yolande led Gabrielle upstairs. "I have something to show you," Yolande whispered, tugging on her friend's arm.

There were two — it was hard to find a word to describe them — blobs, maybe — lying side by side in Yolande's bed. Yolande had stuffed T-shirts and socks underneath the sheets to create human shapes. "That's me," she said, pointing to the blob closest to the door. "That's you. How do you like your hair?"

Gabrielle snorted when she saw Yolande had layered several pairs of black leotards near the top of the second blob. Truth was, it did look like Gabrielle's hair. "Very funny," she said, "but she'll never fall for it."

"Oh, yes she will. Especially since it'll be dark and she'll just peek in like she always does.

There's one more thing," she said, leading Gabrielle to the window.

Gabrielle pushed her head past the curtains and leaned outside. The air felt as hot and dry as the inside of a pizza oven. "Roses," she observed. "Pink. Very pretty."

"For your information, those aren't just any pretty, pink roses. They're climbing roses. Check out what they're climbing on." Yolande was leaning out the window now, too, and pointing toward the hot-pink blossoms.

"A trellis," Gabrielle observed. "Is it new?"

"Kind of. We had this crappy, wooden thing. She replaced it with a wrought-iron one yesterday. A friend of hers from the meditation centre owns a garden store," Yolande explained, raising the screen until it was completely open. Then she hoisted herself up to the window ledge and climbed out.

"What are you doing?" Gabrielle cried out.

"Keep it down, will you?"

Using the trellis as a ladder, Yolande scampered down to the garden. When her feet touched the grass, she looked up at the window and gave Gabrielle a thumbs-up sign. Then, a moment later, as if she was taking part in an obstacle course, Yolande climbed back up. "Pretty cool, huh?" she asked, without pausing to catch her breath.

"But Yolande, what if your mom —"

"What if this? What if that? You know, Gabrielle, you've got to stop all your what if-ing.

It's interfering with your life — and our friendship. Besides, you want to meet Etienne, don't you?"

"Uh-huh," Gabrielle said, "but what if —" She stopped herself.

Yolande grinned. "Just think," she said, "no more having to worry about getting home before dark."

Chapter 4

"Tiffany!" a voice that sounded like liquid honey called from the dance floor. The voice was coming from a tall, broad-shouldered guy with skin the colour of rich milk chocolate. He was doing the Harlem Shake. His knees popped forward as his shoulders rolled backward to the beat.

"Tiffany!" he called again. His head was shaved and he wore baggy, khaki-coloured, low-rise pants and a tight-fitting white tank top, the kind guys called a wife-beater.

Yolande's laughter echoed in the cavernous room. "I forgot to tell you he calls me Tiffany," she said, giggling as she squeezed Gabrielle's hand and began making her way through the thick crowd toward Etienne. He was surrounded by a circle of guys watching him dance. The circle opened to make room for Yolande, or Tiffany.

Gabrielle walked to the edge of the dance floor, stopping to adjust the waist of her tank-top dress.

Though it was 3 a.m., the place was packed. People — most of them in their twenties — were laughing, dancing — and guzzling water. After-hours clubs weren't allowed to sell alcohol, but they sold bottled water and energy drinks. And as Yolande had explained to Gabrielle on the way over, you could buy drugs from the clubbers easily, too.

From outside, The Basement — that was the name of the club — looked like an ordinary basement apartment at the western tip of Monkland Avenue. It had stairs leading down to an aluminum door and narrow windows with steel bars across them. It was the inside that made the place special.

Everything was black or chrome, even the exposed ceiling pipes that gleamed in the darkness. The walls were covered with black satin curtains that swayed when you passed them. There was no furniture, except for the glass DJ's booth and a long, black granite bar at the back of the club.

With so much happening, it was hard to believe most of Montreal was asleep. Just half an hour ago, Yolande and Gabrielle had been sleeping, too. They'd dozed off during the third movie and the second batch of organic popcorn. Luckily, Yolande had set her alarm for 2:30 a.m.

"Why do we have to go out so late — I mean … early?" Gabrielle had asked, rubbing her eyes.

"Etienne works till two. Lousy hours, but security guards make good money," Yolande said, zipping up the black skater's dress that was his latest gift and examining her reflection in the mirror.

Now the music was blaring and Etienne's arms were wrapped around Yolande. They were grinding, dancing so close it was hard to tell their bodies apart. Etienne had thrust his leg between Yolande's thighs and they were pulsing to the beat.

Gabrielle watched them for a few seconds, then let her eyes drop to the floor. Her face was flushed.

"You a friend of Tiffany's?" a man asked.

"Uh, yeah," Gabrielle said, turning toward him. His dark hair was parted down the middle and he wore a pinstripe suit. He looked older than most of the people at the club.

"I'm Henry — and you, you're …" he said, reaching for her hand.

"Gabrielle," she said, letting him take it. His fingers felt cold. "Are you a friend of Etienne's?" she asked, pulling her hand away.

"Sure," he said, "he's introduced me to some of his — friends."

"I guess he has a lot of friends," Gabrielle observed, looking out at the circle of guys still surrounding Yolande and Etienne.

"He's popular, that's for sure," Henry said with a short laugh. "Can you dance the way Tiffany does?" Gabrielle could feel him checking her out, starting with her face, but moving quickly down to her breasts. She crossed her arms over her chest.

"I'm not much of a danc—"

But Henry didn't wait to hear the end of her sentence. Without even saying goodbye, he stood up and headed for the DJ's booth behind the bar.

Yolande waved from the dance floor. "Come here, Gabs!" she called out.

Gabrielle felt more eyes on her as she made her way to the middle of the dance floor. The beat of the music was so strong it pounded in her chest. "You must be Etienne," she said, smiling shyly up at him. You couldn't exactly shake hands with someone who was in the middle of grinding with your best friend.

"Gabrielle," was all Etienne said. For a moment, his brown eyes were glued to hers.

"Having fun?" Yolande asked. "Wanna dance with us?"

"I don't think so," Gabrielle said, rolling her eyes at her friend. "Don't worry about me. I'm not into dancing — I like watching better. Besides, I need water."

"Your friend likes watching?" Etienne said, his fingers playing with the scooped collar on Yolande's dress.

"Oh, Etienne!" Yolande said, wagging her finger in the air, then letting it land on the middle of his bottom lip.

Gabrielle went back to the bar. She tried to throw her shoulders back, the way Yolande did when she walked through a crowded room, but she couldn't manage it for more than a few seconds.

"A bottled water, please," she said to the ponytailed bartender. She raised her voice so he could hear her over the music.

"Seven dollars," he said, handing her a small plastic bottle.

"Seven dollars?!" Gabrielle reached into her purse.

"Yup," the bartender said. His eyes had a blank, expressionless look.

"I'll have water, too. Thanks, Philippe," said a woman, dropping a twenty dollar bill on the granite counter. She stepped closer to Gabrielle. "These places really gouge you on the water," she said.

The woman was thin, with long strawberry-blonde hair. Her face was pretty, but the dark circles under her eyes made her looked tired, even a little worn out. Like she'd been to too many late night parties. "Etienne likes your friend Tiffany," the woman said, as casually as if she was discussing the weather.

"They've been going out for a month," Gabrielle said.

"Going out?" the woman said. She was wearing mauve lipstick. The shade wouldn't have suited most people, but it looked good on her.

"He bought her that dress she's wearing."

"I'm not surprised," the woman said, taking a drag on her cigarette and blowing out a triple ring of smoke. "I should have introduced myself. I'm Hélène."

"Nice to meet you. I'm Gabrielle."

In the distance, Gabrielle could see Yolande

and Etienne walking toward the back of the club. His arm was around her waist and the curtains swayed as they passed.

"Is he nice?" Gabrielle asked.

"Very nice," Hélène said. "All the women fall for him."

"They do?"

Hélène rested her elbows on the bar and leaned forward. Her slinky, black top revealed the pale, rounded tops of her breasts. "I know I did," Hélène whispered.

Chapter 5

"What is it, baby?" Yolande asked.

Etienne wasn't quite himself. Sure, he'd seemed glad to see her, and he'd grinded with her on the dance floor in front of all his friends, but Yolande knew something was wrong. His eyes — she loved his eyes — weren't glowing the way they usually did. It was as if the fire had gone out of them.

When he'd whispered into her ear that he needed to talk to her privately, Yolande felt relieved. Etienne had insisted on knowing everything about her. She'd told him how much she missed her dad, and how she dreamed of becoming a clothing designer.

But all Yolande knew about Etienne was that he worked as a security guard — and that he was nuts for her. In fact, it occurred to her now that when Etienne talked, he mostly talked about her — and how he felt about her. Not that Yolande minded.

One of the things she loved most about Etienne was how good he was at expressing his feelings. He knew how to make her feel important. Like she was worth listening to.

But maybe now Etienne was finally ready to open up and tell her everything about himself. That would bring them even closer, though it was difficult for Yolande to imagine feeling closer to anyone than she felt to Etienne.

Yolande was old enough to know that everyone had problems — even laid-back types like Etienne. But no matter what his problems were, she wanted to be there for him.

Yolande realized that though they'd only been going out for a month, she depended on Etienne. Some people might say that was bad, but Yolande didn't care. She knew it was a sign that she and Etienne were meant to be together. Sure, she had Gabrielle, but having a boyfriend was different. Being with Etienne made her feel grown-up. Sophisticated. And most of all, loved.

Now was her chance to support him through whatever was upsetting him. If she could do that, she was sure he'd love her even more than he already did. The thought sent tiny prickles of anticipation shooting down Yolande's spine. In fact, she could hardly wait to hear what he wanted to tell her. She smiled up at his sullen face.

Once they were behind the satin curtains, Yolande pressed her lips up against Etienne's. She inhaled his smell, a manly smell that reminded her of leather and oranges and cinnamon. He smelled like home. Not a home like the one she shared with her mom; more like the home in her heart.

Etienne made a grunting sound and pushed her away. "I can't," he said in a low, gruff voice she'd never heard before.

"You can't?" She tried to direct his chin down to hers, but Etienne just stared at the wall in front of him. They were in a tiny storage room. Bottles of water and energy drinks lined the shelves.

"What is it, baby?" Yolande asked again. Her voice was gentle, but inside, she was starting to panic. Her throat felt tight and her breathing grew faster. She'd never seen Etienne like this. She was used to having his attention; this sudden change was a shock. She felt like she'd lost something precious.

But when Etienne spoke again, Yolande's anxious feelings disappeared. "Tiffany," he said in that velvety voice she'd fallen in love with when they'd first met, "I need you so much."

"I need you, too, baby," she said, searching for his mouth with her lips.

This time, he kissed her back. But it was a short kiss, and his tongue didn't probe the inside of her mouth the way it usually did.

Yolande leaned in toward Etienne and rocked against him, keeping time with the thump of the music from the other room. "Do you want to go back to your place?" she whispered, sliding her fingers under his T-shirt and letting them trace a small circle on his belly, just under his ribs.

Etienne put his palm over her fingers. "Not tonight. I'm too upset."

"What is it, Etienne?" Yolande asked again. "You have to tell me."

"I can't." Etienne turned away from her. "It's something I need to take care of myself."

That's when Yolande noticed the tears. Tiny droplets that glistened at the outside corners of Etienne's eyes, where the skin was paler. She'd never seen him cry before. And though it broke her heart, she couldn't help feeling glad they were finally getting closer. Etienne was letting her inside. "Oh baby," she said, and for a second, she thought she might cry, too. Now they were really a couple.

Etienne wiped the tears away with the back of his hand. "It's too terrible to tell you," he whispered. "I've never felt so bad about anything."

"Nothing's too bad to tell me," Yolande insisted. "Telling helps. I know it helps when I tell you the stuff that makes me sad. Like about my dad."

Etienne nodded as if he were considering her words. Then he looked up at the ceiling. "I'm in trouble, Tiffany. Big trouble."

"What kind of trouble?" Whatever it was, she'd help him.

"Look, I know it was stupid of me, but I owe money. A lot."

"You do? I thought you make a lot of money." Yolande's eyes landed on her new skater's dress, her Tiffany bracelet, and her stilettos. "Is it because of all the presents you've been buying me?"

"No way, Tiffany," Etienne said, brushing Yolande's hair away from her face. "You deserve all that — and more. No, this is money I owe some guy."

"What guy?"

"His name's Richie. He's a bass player from New York. I met him at the casino. We were playing blackjack and then …" Etienne's voice trailed off.

"How much money?" Yolande had two hundred dollars in her savings account. If Etienne needed it, she'd lend it to him. Give it to him, even. She'd go to the bank first thing in the morning.

"Thousands," Etienne said, looking down at his shoes.

Yolande gasped. She could tell Etienne was ashamed of what he'd done. Anyone could have made the same mistake. "I could give you two hundred," she offered. "You know I'd do anything for you."

Etienne dropped his hands to his sides, so Yolande's fingers were free again to trace circles on his belly. This time, her fingertips circled down to just below his navel.

Etienne moaned softly. "There is something, but I can't ask you to do it."

"What is it? Tell me," Yolande insisted.

"No, Tiffany. I can't. Trust me on this."

"Etienne! You have to tell me!"

"It's Richie …" Etienne looked into Yolande's

eyes. "I told him how gorgeous you are, and ... he ... he wants to take you on a date."

Yolande laughed. "A date? Why would I go on a date with Richie? I'm going out with you."

At first, Etienne didn't say anything. The silence hung in the air between them like a living thing. Etienne opened his mouth to speak, then shut it again. He took a deep breath. "He'd be so happy if he could take you out just once," he whispered. Then Etienne took Yolande's hand and brought it to his heart. "He said if you'd go with him, he'd cancel my debt."

Chapter 6

"The new *Cosmo* just came in the mail. Are you coming here, or should I go to your house?" Gabrielle asked.

"I can't this afternoon," Yolande said.

"It's got an article about twenty-five guaranteed ways to keep your lover coming back for more," Gabrielle explained, giggling into the telephone.

"I told you I can't. I have to do a favour for Etienne."

"What kind of favour?"

Yolande ignored the question. "I'll call you later. I promise."

"Guess that means I'm spending the rest of the afternoon helping Aggie with her collage. I could always cut pictures out of the new *Cosmo* —"

"Don't you dare!" Yolande hissed as she hung up the phone.

Yolande had to admit it: Richie was seriously cute. Ash-blonde hair tied in a long ponytail, green eyes that reminded her of a cat's, and a deep copper tan. He was waiting for her at the Villa Maria métro station in a blue convertible. Just like Etienne said.

Meeting at Villa Maria was Etienne's idea. He said he didn't want her mother or any of the neighbours talking.

"You're gorgeous," Richie said, whistling when she squeezed into the car, which smelled of men's cologne — the expensive kind. Yolande smiled. Who didn't like a compliment — especially one from a cute guy driving a convertible?

She was wearing the black skater's dress. That, too, had been Etienne's idea. "Just keep him happy," he'd whispered in her ear when he'd kissed her goodbye at the after-hours club.

The dress — like the stilettos Etienne had given her — made Yolande feel irresistible. What was that word they used in the romance novels? Ravishing, yes, that was it. Yolande felt ravishing. She didn't mind that Richie was staring at her. In fact, she liked it. Guys always looked at her, and when they did, she felt like she had some magic power over them.

It was Richie's whistle — clear and high-pitched so it sounded like a bird's song — that gave him away. "I can't believe it!" Yolande covered her mouth with her hand. "You're Richie Taylor from Sweet Innocence, right?"

Wait till she told Gabrielle. They'd gawked at his picture in fan magazines since Grade 6. In every shot, they'd noticed, he was with a different woman. All of them blondes with long legs and short skirts.

"Always delighted to meet a new fan," Richie said, taking Yolande's hand and steering it to his lips for a kiss.

Yolande took a deep breath. A bit of stubble on Richie's chin grazed her fingertips.

"So, Tiffany," Richie said, revving the car's engine as they got onto the expressway and headed downtown, "whad'ya say we get ourselves something to eat?" With the other cars racing by and the wind whipping up against the car, he had to raise his voice so she could hear him.

Yolande had eaten lunch three hours ago with her campers — she and Gabrielle worked as counselors at the Y day camp in Notre-Dame-de-Grâce, also known as NDG. But suddenly Yolande felt hungry again. "Sure," she said, eager to get a better look at Richie, but not wanting him to catch her staring.

"You are so beautiful…" Richie sang the words to an old song out loud. His voice was gravelly.

Yolande grinned at her reflection in the passenger mirror. A private concert just for her. The afternoon was turning out to be way more fun than she expected. "I know you play bass, but I didn't know you sing, too," she said.

"I did a little backup when I first got into the biz." He made it sound like a long time ago. But, except for the little lines at the outside corners of his eyes, Richie didn't look that old. Yolande wished she'd paid more attention to the fan magazines.

Richie lifted his hand from the stick shift and let it land on her knee. She could have shaken it off, but she didn't. It was exciting to feel the warm touch of Richie Taylor's fingers.

He took her to the revolving restaurant at the Royal Regency Hotel. "A bottle of Crystal," Richie told the waiter, who was wearing white gloves and carrying a white-linen napkin over one arm.

"Certainly, monsieur," the waiter said. If he noticed Yolande was underage, he didn't say anything.

Yolande sipped her champagne. It had a pleasant, fizzy taste. She tilted her head back and closed her eyes after the second sip. Here she was at one of Montreal's fanciest restaurants, drinking the world's most expensive champagne with a rock star. For all she knew, her picture might end up in a fan magazine, too.

She looked out at the city. From up here, on the top floor of the hotel, she could see the teal waters of the St. Lawrence River, and in the distance, Mont St-Hilaire.

Richie was talking about the band. How they'd just made their fourteenth CD and were touring North America to promote it.

"I guess you meet a lot of girls," Yolande said. The champagne was making her bold.

"Thousands!" Now Richie tilted back his head and laughed. "But most of them are burnt out and jaded. I prefer them sweet and innocent."

Yolande laughed. "Is that why you named the band —"

"You got it," he said, leaning back into his chair and stretching his legs out in front of him so the tips of his sneakers touched Yolande's toes.

"Nice shoes," he said, peering down at the stilettos.

"I got them from —" Yolande stopped herself in mid-sentence. She didn't feel like talking about Etienne.

They ate lobster. The meat had already been loosened from the shell, so they didn't have to crack their lobsters open. When Richie bit into the tail, he squirted Yolande with lobster juice. She used her napkin to wipe the salty brine from her cheek.

"They say shellfish turns girls on," Richie observed, as he signalled the waiter to pour more champagne.

"It does?" Yolande asked, giggling. For a second, the tips of her ears burned. If Etienne was her boyfriend, wasn't it wrong to be talking to some other guy about what turned girls on?

When they stood up to go, Yolande's legs wobbled beneath her. "Not used to champagne, are you, little lady?" Richie asked, wrapping his arm around her waist and letting her lean on his shoulder.

They were the only ones in the elevator. They'd left the convertible with the parking attendant outside, so Yolande was surprised when Richie pressed the button for the eighteenth floor.

"Where we going?" Her voice sounded to her like it was coming from far away.

"To my room," Richie said, as if it was the most natural thing in the world. "So I can show you my bass."

"Are you going to play for me?" she asked, giggling as she looked into his green eyes.

"Sure thing, Tiffany."

She nearly told him her name wasn't Tiffany, but then, she changed her mind. Besides, when Richie opened the door to his room, Yolande suddenly felt like she was someone else. Like she was Tiffany. Like she was the kind of girl who hung out with rock stars.

The bass was lying by the side of the rumpled bed. "Come here," Richie said, tapping a spot next to him on the edge of the bed.

Yolande felt the room spin as she sat down. But Richie didn't play his guitar. Instead, he leaned in to kiss her. His breath smelled like lobster and burned butter, but his lips were soft. She felt his fingers unzip her black dress and reach inside for her breasts, cupping them in his hands.

Yolande knew she shouldn't let him touch her like that, but she didn't want to make him stop either. Everything he was doing felt good. Really good. Warm and cozy and ... exciting. She found herself kissing him back, letting her tongue explore his mouth — the hard edges of his teeth, the upturned end of his tongue.

Then he lay back on the bed and slithered out of his jeans like a snake shedding its skin. She thought about making him stop, but it was too late to go back now. "Just a second, Tiffany," he whispered breathlessly, as he reached for the nightstand drawer.

Yolande heard him remove a condom from its foil wrapper.

Suddenly, Yolande remembered what Etienne had told her: "Just make him happy." Was this what Etienne had meant?

"Oh, Tiffany," Richie moaned as his hand slid up the inside of her thigh. "Your skin feels like silk."

As Richie's face moved in toward hers, she had a better view of the tiny specks of stubble on his chin. They were grey.

Chapter 7

"Whee! This feels good!"

A boy named Toby was sitting in the middle of the parachute, while Yolande and Gabrielle and their other campers held onto the nylon handles and lifted the rainbow-coloured fabric into the air.

"Me next!" voices shouted when the parachute landed on the grass. It amazed Yolande and Gabrielle that their campers never grew tired of this game, though they played it every morning.

Gabrielle was responsible for the four-year-olds; Yolande had the five-year-olds. With the children so close in age, it made sense to do activities together.

"It's important to put things away properly," Gabrielle told the children as they helped fold the parachute.

"Why is it you turn everything into a lesson?" Yolande asked Gabrielle. They were walking toward the playground at the far end of the field, their campers trailing behind them like dutiful ducklings.

"Why is it you're in such a rotten mood today?"

"I'm not."

"Oh, yes you are," Gabrielle said, hooking her arm through Yolande's.

"Yolande, I really need to pee," a little voice called from behind. "Please, can you take me?"

"Do you think you can hold it in a little longer?" Yolande asked. Why was it kids always needed to pee at the most inconvenient times?

"I'll take her," Gabrielle offered.

"I'm not in a bad mood," Yolande said when Gabrielle was back from the bathroom and they were pushing the kids on the swings. "I had too much champagne yesterday is all — Crystal."

"Higher!" shouted the red-headed girl Yolande was pushing. Yolande rolled her eyes.

"What's Crystal?"

"Only the world's most expensive champagne. But the part you won't believe," Yolande lowered her voice, "is who I was drinking it with."

"Etienne?"

"Nope." Yolande crossed her arms over her chest.

"Okay, then, who?"

"Gabrielle! Tina's hogging the shovel," said a little girl who had come to tug on Gabrielle's shorts.

"Tina, let the other kids use the shovel, too!" Gabrielle shouted. Then she turned back to Yolande. "Go on, tell me!"

46

"Richie Taylor."

Gabrielle's mouth fell open and for a second, she forgot to push the swing. "As in Richie Taylor the bass player?"

"You mean Richie Taylor the cool, handsome, incredibly hot bass player. He's friends with Etienne. Etienne wanted me to…" Yolande stopped to find the right words, "keep him entertained."

"Entertained. What were you doing — telling him jokes?"

"Of course not. You know I can't remember jokes. We were … talking … mostly." Yolande looked down at the grass. There was an ant colony right where they were standing. Hundreds of little black ants were scrambling around, doing ant errands. "He was telling me about his band and their new CD. But," Yolande added, lowering her voice, "I kissed him."

"You *kissed* him?" This time, Gabrielle stopped pushing the swing altogether.

"Gabrielle!" the red-headed girl cried out.

"But aren't you going out with Etienne?"

"Yes, I'm going out with him," Yolande said, her lips dropping into a pout, "but that doesn't mean I can't kiss somebody else."

"It doesn't?"

"Of course not. It's not like we're married or anything. Besides, it just sorta happened."

"Are you going to see him again?"

"I don't know. They're flying to Toronto this afternoon."

"Anyway, you shoulda seen his hotel r—" Yolande stopped herself in mid-sentence.

"You saw his hotel room?" Without meaning to, Gabrielle had raised her voice.

"Hotel room! Hotel room!" two of the four-year-olds shouted, jumping up and down as they waited for their turns on the swings.

"Can you two shut up?" Yolande barked.

The little girls fell silent. "You're not supposed to say 'shut up,'" one of them said at last. The other one just stared blankly at Yolande.

"Look, I'm sorry. I shouldn't have said it," Yolande sputtered. "Do you wanna take your turns on the swings?" she asked.

"Okay," the girls said, without moving from their spots.

They lifted their campers down from the swings and gave the other two a turn. "I wasn't there for long. It was no big deal," Yolande said at last. She gave the swing a strong push. "Besides, you shouldn't judge."

"You could have gotten into a lot of trouble," Gabrielle said softly.

"Some of us aren't afraid of a little trouble."

"I didn't say a little — I said a lot."

* * *

When camp ended at 3 p.m., Etienne was waiting at the gate outside the Y. Yolande reached for Gabrielle's hand when she spotted him. "I hope he's not upset," she whispered.

"He doesn't look upset."

"The thing is," Yolande said, sidling up to Gabrielle, "I guess I do feel a little guilty about Richie. Things just kind of got out of hand."

Gabrielle looked at her friend. "Hey," she said, "I don't want to be judgmental. Like you said, it's not like you and Etienne are married. Plus, it was just a kiss, right?" She patted Yolande's elbow.

Etienne was doing a shuffle on the sidewalk. His hands were behind his back and his head was rocking to some imaginary beat.

"Do you want me to stick around?" Gabrielle asked.

"No, I'm okay on my own. How 'bout I meet you at the lockers in ten minutes? That way we can still walk home together."

Gabrielle waved at Etienne before she headed back into the Y.

"Aren't you supposed to be working?" Yolande called out as she walked up to Etienne. Her voice sounded happier than she felt. She dropped her hands to her sides and dug her nails into the fleshy part of her palms. She'd gotten carried away last night. She'd never meant to hurt Etienne.

But Etienne wasn't acting hurt. "I wanted to see my baby before I went to work!" With one hand, he pulled her toward him, holding her about a foot away and gazing into her eyes. Yolande made herself smile. "You're the best," he said.

Yolande blushed. "I am?" She didn't feel like

she was the best, that was for sure. No, she felt more like the worst girlfriend on planet Earth. "You sure everything's okay?" she whispered. She hoped he didn't notice her voice was shaking.

"Everything's amazing," Etienne said. Then he brought out what he'd been hiding: a bouquet of long-stemmed red roses. A dozen of them.

Yolande buried her nose in the flowers and smiled. Then she stood up on her tip-toes and kissed him. For a split second, she thought about Richie Taylor and how he tasted like burnt butter. That made her kiss Etienne even harder.

He put his hands around her waist, lifted her up into the air and spun her around.

"Careful!" Yolande cried out, laughing. "You're squashing my roses!"

Chapter 8

A neighbour's striped cat meowed loudly as Yolande climbed down the trellis, taking little steps because she was wearing her miniskirt. "Shh," she told the cat when it hissed at her accusingly.

Etienne was waiting at the corner. He was holding a small box wrapped in gold paper and tied with a red ribbon.

"Etienne!" Yolande giggled, putting her arm around his waist, "how come you're always spoiling me?"

"How do you know it's for you?" he asked, leaning in for a kiss.

"Mmm," Yolande said, kissing him back. "Who else would that little box be for?"

"Could be for one of my other girls," Etienne said, tweaking the end of her nose.

Yolande threw her head back and laughed. Laughing felt good. Yolande had been feeling stressed out since her date with Richie Taylor. The worst part was she didn't have anyone to talk to about how she was feeling. If Gabrielle had freaked out when Yolande told her she'd kissed Richie, she didn't like to imagine how Gabrielle would react if she knew the whole story.

"You deserve to be spoiled," Etienne said, stopping under the yellow light of a street lamp to give her the present. "You're gorgeous and fun — and you don't have a daddy to spoil you."

"You're so sweet," Yolande said as she unwrapped the package. For a second, she felt tears sting her eyes. She'd only told Etienne a little about her dad — how sad she was that her memories of him had begun to fade — but it was just like Etienne to remember, to pay attention to the details.

Yolande squealed when she saw the peach-coloured box. Inside was a glass bottle, shaped like a female torso. Jean Paul Gaultier perfume. How had Etienne known she wanted it? She removed the stopper and inhaled the perfume's sweet scent.

"Go ahead, Tiffany, put some on."

Etienne grinned as she dabbed the perfume on her wrists. Suddenly, Yolande remembered her dad's smile when he'd walked into the house one day and found her playing dress-up. She'd been parading around in one of her mom's summer dresses and carrying her mom's old purse.

Etienne grabbed Yolande's hands and brought them up to his nose. "Yum," he growled. He placed her hands on the V-neck of her T-shirt, pressing down for a second before letting go. Then he bent his face down and nuzzled the spot. "Yum," he growled again.

"Etienne!"

"You make me crazy!"

"Are we going to your place?"

"Not tonight. You and me are invited to a party. And you're going to be the sexiest, sweetest-smelling lady there."

Etienne knew exactly how to make Yolande feel good. And if he knew anything about what had happened in Richie Taylor's hotel room, he wasn't letting on.

A cab was waiting at the next corner. "St-Paul Street in Old Montreal," Etienne told the driver.

With so little traffic, they were in Old Montreal in ten minutes. The cab pulled up in front of a grey stone church. "You're taking me to a party in a church?" Yolande asked as she stepped out onto the cobblestone street.

"It used to be a church," Etienne explained, holding the door for her. He used the buzzer outside the lobby, which, judging from the tall ceilings and stained-glass windows, had once been the chapel.

Yolande followed Etienne up to a huge loft overlooking the Old Port. People, all of them older than her, were chatting on leather sofas; others were out on the terrace, looking out at the ships or up at the stars. One couple made moaning sounds as they kissed, oblivious to onlookers. The gold clasp of the woman's pearl necklace gleamed against the night sky.

The guests didn't look anything like the kids who drank beer and played Truth or Dare at the house parties Yolande was used to.

Yolande let herself enjoy the feeling of people watching her and Etienne walk through the crowd. Just having a boyfriend made her feel special. Besides, she knew they made a striking couple.

"You smell good," a man whispered as his elbow grazed hers.

Etienne caught her eye and smiled. A waiter passed with a tinkling tray of drinks. Etienne reached for a Smirnoff Ice and passed it to Yolande. She took a long, slow sip. Already, she felt more comfortable.

Etienne led her toward a muscular-looking man standing by the window. "Josh," Etienne said, giving him a high-five, "Meet Tiffany. Tiffany, Josh. This is Josh's place."

"It's great," Yolande said, extending her hand and hoping she didn't sound like a kid.

"You were right," Josh told Etienne. "She's beautiful — and young."

Yolande blushed. It was a compliment, but the way Josh talked about her when she was standing right there made her feel invisible.

Another man slapped Etienne's shoulder. "Hey, Etienne. How's business?" he asked in a booming voice. Like Josh, you could tell from his bulging biceps that he spent a lot of time at the gym.

"Things are good, Tony. Real good," Etienne said. "This here's Tiffany."

Yolande inched closer to Etienne as Tony checked her out, his eyes moving slowly down her legs. Though she was used to men looking at her, she didn't expect it when she was with Etienne. But Etienne didn't seem to notice. His eyes were scanning the room, as if he was looking for some-one else.

Just then, his pager beeped. He stepped away from Yolande as he reached into his pocket. "Jesus," he said, his voice dropping when he looked at the pager. "This could be a problem."

"Maybe we should go," Yolande suggested.

Etienne raised one finger to his chin as if he was considering the possibility. "No. It'd be easier if I left you here while I go straighten this thing out. Josh and Tony'll look after you. Won't you, guys?"

"It'd be our pleasure," Josh said.

"Absolutely," Tony added.

Etienne squeezed Yolande's hand. When he rushed out of the loft a couple of minutes later, he didn't even stop to look back at her.

Yolande bit her lip as she smiled up at Josh and Tony. Sometimes, Etienne wasn't all that perfect.

Chapter 9

"Care for a tequila?" Tony asked. The three of them were sitting on chrome barstools that were more comfortable than they looked.

Yolande figured she might as well make the best of things and party a little before Etienne got back. She watched Josh as he ran his tongue along the skin between his thumb and finger, sprinkled it with salt, and licked the spot again before downing a shooter of tequila.

"Your turn," he said, passing her the shaker of salt.

The tequila burned the inside of her throat.

She bit into a wedge of lime Tony handed her.

The woman with the pearl necklace walked by. Now she was holding hands with a tall guy — not the one she'd been kissing on the balcony. "What happened to her boyfriend?" Yolande asked, suddenly realizing she was talking too loudly.

Josh smiled as the couple headed for an alcove

under the glass stairway that divided the loft. "Oh, her," he said. "Let's just say she's more into pleasure than commitment."

Yolande twirled a strand of her pale hair between her fingers and tried to imagine what it would be like to care more about pleasure than commitment. When Josh and Tony laughed, Yolande joined in.

"Let's drink to pleasure!" Tony said, refilling Yolande's glass.

"Let's make this a little more fun." Josh took the shooter from Tony's hand and put it back on the counter. "Did you ever play 'I Never?'" he asked Yolande.

"It's a drinking game, right?" Yolande didn't want to admit she'd never played it.

"We ask if you ever did something. If you did, you down a shooter." When Tony took the bottle from the counter, the tequila made a swishing sound.

"I just thought of one," Josh began, turning to Yolande. "Did you ever skip school?"

Yolande rolled her eyes. "Of course I did."

"Drink up!" Josh handed her the glass.

"My turn," Yolande said. "Did you ever get so drunk you threw up?" she asked Tony.

"Never. I know my limits," Tony said, grinning as he eyed the tequila bottle. "I got one for you. Did you ever cheat on your boyfriend?"

Yolande blushed. For a second, she remembered Richie Taylor. "N-no —" she stammered. "Never."

"I don't know about you, Tony, but I think she's lying. You wouldn't lie to us, now would you, Tiffany?"

Yolande could feel Josh's pale eyes watching her.

"You'd better have that tequila. Just in case." Tony laughed as he refilled her glass. Yolande's tongue felt heavy as she emptied the shooter.

"Did you ever have sex in a bathroom?" Yolande asked Josh, giggling as she looked into his eyes. She couldn't believe she'd asked the question. Maybe she'd had too much tequila.

"Who hasn't?" Josh asked, pouring himself a shooter and downing it in one gulp. He paused to consider his next question. "Did you ever blow a guy?"

It was a question that would usually have embarrassed her, but now Yolande just laughed. "Who hasn't?" she said. "No more tequila for me," she added, pushing away the glass Josh was passing her.

"You have to," Josh said. "It's the rules of the game."

Now Yolande's head was beginning to feel heavy. She gulped as she finished the third glass of tequila.

"Did you ever have sex with two guys?" Tony asked.

Yolande lifted her hands to her cheeks. Her face felt hot.

"Hey buddy, can't you see you're embarrassing

her?" Josh nudged Tony's elbow.

"That's the point, isn't it?" Tony said.

That made them all laugh. It felt like a part of Yolande was outside herself, observing. She heard herself laugh and watched herself joke with Josh and Tony, touching their hands or their chests when they made her laugh.

"How'd you like to see the rest of the condo?" Josh asked.

"Isn't this it?" Yolande said. She was glad the game of "I Never" seemed to be over.

"There's a VIP room," Josh said. "For very important princesses."

"And I'm a princess, right?"

"Damned right you are," Tony said. "Come on, we'd like to show you," he added, getting up from his stool and coming closer to Yolande. She could smell the tequila on his breath.

"Okay." Yolande's legs wobbled when she stood up. She tried to steady herself by reaching for the counter, but somehow she missed it and lost her footing.

"I think you need a little help," Josh said, grabbing her elbow. Tony took hold of her other arm. Everything was moving in slow motion. Yolande could feel the other guests craning their necks ever so slowly to look at her as she stumbled upstairs, propped up between the two guys.

The glass stairway led to what Josh had called his VIP room. It was shaped like an octagon and a line of chunky ivory-coloured candles glowed in the window. They gave off an aroma of vanilla as they burned. "It's gorcheous," Yolande said, giggling at her mistake. "I mean … gor-cheous." Why couldn't she get the word right?

"Princesses like it up here," Josh said, sitting down in a white leather armchair. "There's room for two," he said, smiling up at Yolande. His teeth were very white. "Come watch the ships."

She laughed when Josh pulled her onto his lap. "I'm looking after you," he said. "Just like Etienne asked me to."

"Just like Etienne asked you to," Yolande repeated, nodding her chin.

Tony was at the window, adjusting the vertical blinds. Now he turned to look at Yolande and Josh.

"You two look cozy," he said. "What do you say I join you?"

A moment later, Tony was perched on the end of the armchair. Josh was running his fingers through Yolande's hair. Tony had slipped off one of her stilettos. "Nice feet," he said, and then he kissed one of her toes.

Yolande giggled. The sound seemed to come from far away. What was it Josh had said before about pleasure? She tried to remember, but she couldn't. Then for a moment, Yolande saw herself from outside again. She was with two good-looking, built guys who wanted to be with her at the same time. She'd never felt so — so — hot. So wanted.

But afterwards, when Josh and Tony left to go

downstairs and Yolande was picking her bra and panties off the wood floor, she didn't feel so hot. Her head ached and she was pretty sure she was about to vomit.

Chapter 10

The ringing hurt her head. She reached an arm from under the sheets and grabbed the phone. She'd paged Etienne, so it had to be him phoning her back.

"There's no way I'm going to camp today," Yolande croaked into the receiver. From her bed, she could see her reflection in the oval mirror over her bureau. Her hair was stringy and there were dark half moons under her eyes. She looked gross. Yolande shut her eyes.

"You have to," Etienne told her. "Working at that Y is your first real job. You need to show them you're responsible."

At least her dad couldn't see her. When Yolande had come in at 4 a.m., she'd done only one thing before collapsing on her bed — she'd turned her dad's picture around to face the wall so that all she could see now was the edge of the frame and the cardboard backing. She knew she wouldn't have been able to bear waking up to her father's smiling face, his greyish-blue eyes so like her own.

"My head hurts," Yolande moaned, kicking off her bedspread and rubbing her temples. "There's no way I can deal with eight five-year-olds today."

"Of course you can, Tiffany. You're Supergirl."

Yolande ignored the compliment. She took a deep breath and said what she'd wanted to since she'd picked up the phone to page Etienne. She couldn't go on pretending things were okay. "We need to talk about what happened last night."

"Look, Tiffany, I'm really sorry I didn't get back to the condo. Things got … complicated. But I talked to Josh, and he told me he sent you home by cab."

"That's not what we need to talk about." Even to her own ears, Yolande's voice sounded tinny and shrill.

"Tiffany, baby, you don't have to worry about anything. Everything's okay. You got that?"

Yolande didn't answer. What was he talking about? How could things be okay?

"Repeat after me: 'Everything's okay.'"

"Everything's okay," Yolande said at last. Funny how saying the words made her feel a little better. But just a little. She opened her eyes and rolled one shoulder back, then the other. Her body ached.

"Listen, why don't you come over to my place after you finish camp today — then we can talk and … whatever …"

Yolande sighed. She hadn't been to Etienne's

apartment since camp had started. If she knew she was going to see him, she might be able to get through the day. Yolande dragged herself out of bed and stepped into her slippers. "Okay," she said into the telephone. "I give up. I'll go to camp. But only because I get to see you later."

Etienne blew a kiss into the phone. "That's my girl."

Just as Yolande was about to put the phone back on the cradle, she heard the beeping sound of Etienne's pager going off in his apartment. How could Etienne stand getting paged all the time?

She tugged her T-shirt over her head.

* * *

To make matters worse, it was pouring. That heavy rain that comes down in thick, grey diagonal lines and leaves puddles too big to cross without soaking your feet.

"Wonderful for my roses," Yolande's mother said, gazing out the kitchen window as Yolande sat down at the table. "I made you a strawberry and wheat germ shake wi—"

"With lecithin," Yolande muttered. "You make me that every single morning." She reached for the movie section of the newspaper so she could hide behind it and escape her mother's cheerfulness.

"Imagine having a mom who makes sure her daughter gets her daily dose of lecithin!" Mrs. Owen said brightly.

Yolande pretended to read the movie listings.

Rain wasn't only good for the roses. It meant arts and crafts. Tissue-paper flowers, macaroni art — and a room full of little sticky fingers all wanting to touch her. How could the day get any worse?

"There's an umbrella by the door," her mother said, putting on her raincoat. When she leaned over to kiss Yolande, she stopped to look at her. Yolande turned away. For a second, she wondered whether her mother could tell what she'd been up to the night before. Suddenly, Yolande saw an image of herself with Josh and Tony. She blinked to make the picture go away. How could she have been so dumb? If only Etienne hadn't had to leave the party!

Yolande's mother bit her lip and made the tsking sound she sometimes made. Yolande's heart thumped inside her chest.

"You haven't been skipping your vitamin B complex, have you?"

Yolande found it hard not to laugh.

* * *

The Y smelled like one gigantic locker room. Yolande and Gabrielle had to cross over a long, snaking line of rubber boots to reach the lobby where their campers were waiting.

"Yo-yo! Gabs!" the four- and five-year-olds shouted, swarming the girls.

Gabrielle squatted down so she could hug two of her campers.

Yolande groaned. She couldn't stand the feeling of the children pressing in on her, their skin still damp from the rain.

"Do me a favour and don't go asking if I'm in a bad mood today," she told Gabrielle once the crowd of children had thinned. "I'm PMSing big time."

Just then, Lydia, the head counsellor, bustled into the lobby, blowing her whistle to announce her arrival. Yolande blocked her ears and wished she were still in bed, the covers pulled over her head.

"We're doing macaroni art today," Lydia announced as excitedly as if she was telling the counsellors they'd won the lottery. Then she handed them each a bag of dried noodles, a packet of cardboard, and two bottles of white glue.

"Macaroni art?" Nick asked. He and his twin brother, William, were counsellors at the camp, too. Yolande and Gabrielle had met them at training before camp started. The twins had the same carrot-coloured hair and freckles. If it weren't for the difference in height — Nick was several inches taller than his brother — it would have been hard to tell them apart. "Macaroni paintings are old," Nick said.

"Our grandparents did macaroni paintings when they went to summer camp," William added.

"Our grandparents went to summer camp?" Nick had missed his brother's sarcasm.

"I've met with my campers," William said, ignoring his brother as he continued speaking to Lydia, but loudly enough so that everybody else in the room could hear, "and they'd rather play stick hockey in the gym."

Lydia was about to use her whistle again, but then she seemed to change her mind. Yolande and Gabrielle exchanged smiles.

"Yay! Stick hockey!" the kids in the lobby shouted. "We want stick hockey!"

So instead of arts and crafts, there were two games of stick hockey, followed by a picnic lunch in the lobby, and then swimming lessons in the indoor pool. It was a long, busy day, but at least they'd been spared macaroni art.

When camp was finally over, Gabrielle waited with Yolande at the bus shelter on Monkland Avenue When the twins walked by, they took off their baseball caps and bowed. "Have a good rest of the afternoon, ladies," William said.

Gabrielle blushed. "You, too," she said.

Yolande ignored them.

"They're cute," Gabrielle told Yolande as the brothers headed down a side street.

"They're babies."

* * *

Etienne danced to the front door of his apartment. Rap music blared from inside. He peered down the hallway, then whisked Yolande inside.

He scooped her in his arms, lifting her off the floor, and kissed her. "Hey, Tiffany," he said, beaming into her eyes.

The tiredness Yolande had been battling all day began to lift. She'd been an idiot, but she wanted to start over and be a good girlfriend, the kind of girlfriend a guy like Etienne deserved. "Everything's okay," she reminded herself as she tried to relax in his strong arms.

As Etienne led her to the couch, past his shiny, chrome stereo equipment and his shelves of DVDs and CDs, Yolande sniffed the air. "What smells so good?"

"*Grillot* with *sauce ti malice*. I made you a Creole dinner."

"Wow," Yolande said. This was the first time a guy had cooked for her. Not counting her dad, of course.

When she saw how Etienne had set the table using white china dishes with gold rims and matching white-and-gold candlesticks, she only felt guiltier. "I didn't know you like to cook," she said.

"I don't. But I like you. A lot." They were back on the couch and Etienne was rubbing her neck and shoulders, pressing his fingertips into the hollow spots between her shoulder blades.

Yolande sighed. She hadn't realized there were knots in her neck. Not looking at Etienne made it easier for Yolande to say what she had to say. "Something … bad … happened last night," she

68

began, stumbling over the words, but relieved that at least she'd started the conversation. She had to come clean to Etienne. "With Josh and Tony."

Etienne let go of her shoulders. "No one told me it was bad," he whispered. "In fact, I heard it was pretty good."

Yolande couldn't bear to turn around and face him. "You mean you know?" she asked.

If he knew, why had he invited her over to his place? And why had he gone to the trouble of making her dinner? And why wasn't he angry? Or jealous? None of this was making any sense.

"Of course I know. But don't worry. I'm not upset." Etienne was rubbing her shoulders again. "You love me, don't you, baby?"

Yolande felt tears beginning to form at the corners of her eyes. "You know I do. I love you so much, Etienne. You're the only guy I want to be with." The tears followed, hot and wet, and she used the back of her hand to wipe them away.

Yolande felt Etienne get up from the couch. A moment later, he sat down again, closer to Yolande, so his face was only an inch or two from hers. He dabbed her cheeks with his hand. "Listen. I'm glad you had a good time last night! I love you, baby. And when you love someone, you want them to have a good time — to experience life. So long as I'm the one you love. That's all that matters. Do you understand what I'm saying?"

Yolande sniffled and tried to concentrate on Etienne's words. Maybe he was right. If you love someone, you should let them experience life. Shouldn't you? But Yolande knew she couldn't take it if Etienne had sex with someone else. Just thinking about it made her head and chest hurt. Did that mean she didn't really love him? But she did love him! She knew she did! Why did love have to be so confusing?

"You are the one I love," Yolande said, wrapping her arms around Etienne's neck and looking into his dark eyes. "The only one."

Chapter 11

"Does it hurt?" Gabrielle asked.

"It's like he's pinching me. A lot," Yolande muttered. She was straddling a chair while Rob, the tattoo artist, worked on the small of her back.

The needle was tiny, but it was attached to a six-inch stainless steel holder. Gabrielle winced when she looked at it. "Here, squeeze my hand," she told Yolande.

"I think you're taking this harder than I am," Yolande said as she squeezed Gabrielle's hand, only to release it quickly. "Ick, your fingers are all sweaty."

"Try not to move," Rob told Yolande as he adjusted the tube of blue dye connected to the needle, "this is delicate work."

Rob had even more tattoos than that basketball player Dennis Rodman. In fact, the tattoos on Rob's forearms and lower legs looked more like clothing than skin. Most were of dragons breathing fire or waving their scaly tails in the air.

Yolande was having the letters E. G — Etienne's initials — tattooed in tiny Gothic script on the middle of her lower back. "Just over the crack in my butt," she'd told Rob when she and Gabrielle had gone to scout out tattoo and piercing shops the week before.

Gabrielle had tried talking Yolande out of it. But in the end, Gabrielle had shrugged her shoulders and offered to come along. "If you're really going to do it, you have to make sure the place is super clean and they don't reuse their needles. Otherwise, you could catch hepatitis — or even AIDS," Gabrielle warned.

"Why am I not surprised there's a lesson in this?" Yolande asked.

In the end, they decided on Rush, a tattoo and piercing shop on the western edge of downtown. The place smelled of antiseptic, the artists wore latex gloves and Rob had insisted on seeing ID "You're over eighteen, right?" he'd asked, before getting Yolande to fill out a form asking for her name, address, height, and weight and whether she had any allergies.

"Of course I am," Yolande had said, pulling out the fake ID card Etienne had made her and meeting Rob's gaze. She'd learned that if you were going to lie, it helped if you looked whomever you were lying to right in the eye. Gabrielle said she'd never be able to do it. "I'd start laughing or something," she'd said.

Prices at Rush were higher than at the sleazy tattoo parlors near St-Laurent Boulevard. The tattoo was going to cost fifty dollars, though it was only the size of a quarter. Yolande told Gabrielle she wanted it to look subtle.

"Yeah, sure," Gabrielle had said. "Good luck trying to convince me that getting your boyfriend's initials tattooed over your butt is subtle."

"Well, subtle enough so my mom won't see it."

From the front, Rush looked like a regular store, with racks of silver body jewelry and T-shirts for sale. But at the back there were two tattooing cubicles and a glassed-in piercing room, where customers with strong stomachs could watch the body piercers at work.

What surprised Yolande most was the clients. Not one of them looked like a trucker or a member of some biker gang; they looked more like the kinds of people who dropped their kids off at the Y and bought groceries on Monkland.

"If you and E. G. ever break up," Rob told Yolande when he'd finished the tattoo and was helping her up from the chair, "we could turn his initials into a flower or a fairy."

Yolande gave Rob an icy look. "We're not going to break up. Ever. We're totally in love. Totally."

Rob looked like he was sorry he'd even mentioned it. "Well then, let's have a look." He led Yolande to a full-length mirror at the other side of the cubicle. "It's a little swollen, but that'll go away. I'm going to put on a gauze strip. You can take it off in an hour. After that, you've gotta keep the tattoo clean — and if you don't want it to fade, stay out of the sun for the next two weeks."

Yolande nodded as she pressed her body up to mirror to inspect the tattoo. It was red and puffy, but the initials were clear: E. G. "I love it!" she said.

"What'd you do to get a fifty dollar bill?" Gabrielle asked Yolande when they were at the front cash and she pulled the red bill from her wallet.

"Etienne gave it to me. He insisted on paying for the tattoo. It makes sense since he's the one who thought of it."

"Did he say anything about his plans to get your initials tattooed over his butt?" Gabrielle asked as they headed for the Guy métro station.

Yolande ignored the question. "Did I tell you about this really cool pair of Miss Sixty jeans he bought me? And the red striped halter top that goes with it?"

Gabrielle turned to look at Yolande. "Imagine what all that must've cost him."

"He really loves me," Yolande said.

"Don't you ever feel uncomfortable accepting all that stuff from him?"

"No, I don't." The question seemed to surprise Yolande. "Why should I?"

"I was just wondering is all. I think if it were me, I'd feel uncomfortable. Like I owed him something. Besides, don't you ever wonder how he can afford all those presents on a security guard's salary?"

"I told you his job pays really well," Yolande muttered under her breath. Then suddenly, she stopped walking and took hold of Gabrielle's elbow, pinning it down with her hand. "Don't you ever get tired of acting like you're better than everyone else?" Yolande's eyes narrowed as she spoke.

"I was just asking a question is all." Gabrielle shook her elbow free. They were standing on the sidewalk outside the métro station. Passersby had to circle around them to get inside.

"You know what you should do?" Yolande asked Gabrielle.

"What?"

"Get a life!" With that, Yolande turned her back and marched back up Guy Street.

Chapter 12

He wasn't watching the security cameras. He didn't even notice her come in through a revolving door at the front of the IBM building. He was too busy reading. Which wasn't what Yolande had expected.

She hadn't planned to come. After the argument with Gabrielle, she'd just kept walking, too angry to do anything else, and ended up here. She hoped Etienne wouldn't mind her showing up unannounced.

When he finally looked up from his desk, he seemed puzzled. Maybe it was because he was distracted by his book. "Can I hel— Hey baby, whatcha doin' here?" His voice echoed in the huge granite lobby. They were alone except for one woman waiting at a nearby bank of elevators. The elevator made a chiming sound when the doors opened to let her in.

Etienne looked different in his uniform — still handsome, but more serious. He was wearing a plain khaki-coloured shirt, done up nearly to the top, with matching pants, but not the baggy kind he usually wore.

Yolande reached for the book. *No Exit* by Jean Paul Sartre. It was one of Madame Leroux's favourite plays. "A classic work of existentialism," she'd told them. "We'll be reading it next year in grade eleven English."

She tried to remember what Madame Leroux had said about existentialism: We're born alone and we die alone; it's up to each of us to make life meaningful.

"I got the tattoo," Yolande said, turning around and bending over from the waist so Etienne could see it.

He whistled. "Looks great! Hey babe, why don't you come stand over here?" Etienne pointed to a spot next to him. "Unless you want management to catch you on camera showing off that tattoo!" He pointed up at one of the closed circuit monitors.

"Oops," Yolande said, moving away quickly so her image disappeared from the screen. "Gabs came with me to get the tattoo, but then we had a fight. I didn't know what else to do, so I came here."

"Poor baby," Etienne said, brushing a strand of pale hair away from her eyes. "What did you fight about?"

Yolande looked down at her feet. "About you — sort of."

Etienne didn't seem surprised. "Gabrielle doesn't approve of me? Is that it?"

"She doesn't approve of me," Yolande said in a small voice.

"What does that mean?"

"She thinks it's wrong of me to accept presents from you."

"What matters is what you think."

"I think you're amazing."

Etienne grinned. "You remember that, Tiffany," he whispered into her ear.

"Etienne, are you really sure you can afford all that stuff you buy me?" Yolande turned around to make sure there was no one listening. "Even after the gambling debt …"

"Don't worry about it, babe. I've got things under control."

Yolande didn't want to worry, but Gabrielle's questions kept buzzing in her head, like a fly that wouldn't go away. "Security guards don't earn that much money, do they?"

"Sure we do," Etienne said, straightening his shoulders, which made his shirt pull across his chest.

"On my way over, I was thinking how you know everything there is to know about me." Yolande reached for Etienne's hand. "But you never told me your story."

"I never knew you liked stories."

"I guess I do. But I never read *No Exit*." Yolande looked down at the book on the desk in front of them.

"I think you'd like it. It's about this guy,

Garcin, and two women. They're stuck together forever. That's why it's called *No Exit*."

"It sounds depressing," Yolande said.

"Most stories are."

"Is yours?"

Etienne turned away, but he kept talking. "Yeah," he said, "it's depressing, but at least it's got a happy ending."

"Happy endings don't work. At least, that's what Madame Leroux says: they're not realistic."

"Who's she? Your teacher?"

"Uh-huh."

"I went to school in Haiti, but only till fourth grade."

"What happened after that?"

"A lot. My sister Solange took sick. No one knew what she had. There wasn't money for a doctor. So I went to work." He said all this without emotion, as if he were checking off items on a grocery list.

"What kind of work?"

"The only kind of work there is in Haiti. Farming. Now you're gonna ask me what we farmed, aren't you?"

Yolande nodded. "What did you farm?"

"Mangos. What do you know about Haiti?"

"Not much," Yolande admitted. "I think there was a revolution. Last year, there were terrible floods."

"Do you know how poor Haitians are?"

"I … think I do."

"Except for what I send her, my mother lives on six dollars a week. She's got four more kids at home. They live in a one-room hut. There's a thatched roof," his voice wandered off, as if he was picturing that house on the other side of the ocean. "When it rains, they sleep under the bed to keep dry." Etienne watched Yolande's face turn pale. "Is that what you wanted to know?"

For a moment, Yolande didn't say a word. "What happened to Solange?"

"She died."

The words sounded as if Etienne had spit them out and left them on the desk next to Sartre's play.

"I'm sorry."

"We didn't get her to the doctor in time. There was something wrong with her lungs. She could not stop coughing. And then she just died. That taught me something."

"What?" Yolande's voice was barely louder than a whisper.

"It takes money to survive."

"Is that why you work so hard?"

Etienne laughed. "That's right," he said, "that's exactly why I work so hard."

"What about your dad?" Yolande asked. "What's he like?"

"Don't ask me," Etienne said, turning to peer out at the street. When he spoke again, Yolande noticed his fists were clenched. "I never had the pleasure of meeting the dude. If my mom had treated him better, maybe he'd have stuck around."

Yolande stroked the side of Etienne's face. "What about the happy ending?"

Etienne unclenched his fists. "The happy ending is that because of what I send her, my mom just bought a tin sheet for under her roof. The happy ending is I'm here. With you."

All Yolande's problems suddenly seemed small and unimportant compared to what Etienne and his family had been through. She had so much to be grateful for. Most of all, she had Etienne. "I want to help you," she said.

Etienne sighed. "You're already helping me — more than you know." Then he looked deep into her eyes, so deep Yolande felt her insides quiver.

When Etienne spoke again, his voice was very quiet. "Listen, babe. Josh phoned this morning. He wanted to know if he could see you tonight. I said I was pretty sure I could arrange it."

Chapter 13

"You've got terrific hair. So blonde and silky." Marcel sighed as he ran his fingers through it. "It just needs a trim. We'll get rid of the split ends and freshen up your look."

"Great," Yolande said, forcing herself to smile up at Marcel's reflection in the mirror.

It was Saturday morning and Yolande had never felt so tired in her life. Her neck was stiff and her whole body, even her eyelids, felt heavy. She hadn't gotten home until nearly 5 a.m., and even then she'd had trouble falling asleep. She'd kept remembering her night out with Josh. Actually, it was more of a night in.

They'd eaten Chinese takeout on his terrace, straight from the cardboard cartons. He'd laughed when she showed him the message inside her fortune cookie: "Your life is like a road with many twists and turns."

"Here, look at mine," he'd said, moving his

chair closer. "'You will have your true desire.' Now ain't that the truth? My true desire was to have you to myself tonight. No sharing. And then, like magic," Josh snapped his fingers, "here you are."

Yolande told herself she was experiencing life. Just like Etienne said she should. So how come she didn't feel happier about it?

What she'd most wanted to do this morning was stay in bed with the covers pulled over her head, but Etienne had phoned and woken her up. "Something tells me my baby needs some pampering," he'd said. "So I went ahead and booked you a day at Monkland Spa. Can you be there by ten?"

Yolande had only read about women who spent their days at spas, being fussed over like Cleopatra. Besides, Etienne was right. She needed pampering, all right. So she'd tugged on her jeans, guzzled the strawberry, wheat germ, and lecithin shake her mom had left on the kitchen table, and hurried over to Monkland.

The spa was as busy as Central Station at rush hour. A row of women were waiting to have their hair washed at the sinks near the back of the salon; others were drying their hair under heat lamps; and another three were getting highlights. Locks of their hair were wrapped in tinfoil and sticking out at odd angles, making them look like aliens.

Yolande had already had a manicure, pedicure, and facial. After Marcel finished her hair, she was going downstairs for a mineral bath and a massage. Etienne had taken care of everything. He'd chosen her treatments and even left enough money to cover tips. As usual, he'd remembered the details.

Yolande watched as Marcel snipped at her hair, a look of total concentration on his face. Her fingernails, just visible at the edge of the cotton smock she was wearing, were polished a silvery pink.

Yolande tried to relax into the chair, but she couldn't. She kept readjusting herself, trying to get comfortable. Most of all, she was determined to avoid her reflection in the mirror. Pleasure over commitment. That was what that woman she'd seen at Josh's party believed in. Etienne had said he didn't own her, and that it was important for her to experience different guys. But just like she couldn't get comfortable in the chair, the stuff going on in her own life made her feel uncomfortable, too.

"Excuse me," a woman in the next chair interrupted Yolande's thoughts. "What colour nail polish have you got on?"

Another hairdresser was trimming the woman's strawberry blonde bangs. Yolande noticed a slinky black skirt and long legs peeping out from under the woman's smock. "It's Kiss-Me Pink," Yolande said, stretching out her fingers like a cat extending its nails.

Yolande studied the woman's reflection in the mirror in front of them. She had on mauve lipstick and there were dark circles under her eyes. She looked even more tired than Yolande felt.

"My name's Hélène." The woman tried not to move her head. "I've seen you at The Basement."

Marcel picked his blow dryer up from the counter, stopping to untangle the electrical cord. "Is your colour natural?" Hélène raised her voice so Yolande would hear her over the sound of the blow dryer.

"Uh-huh, it is."

When Marcel finished, Yolande's hair was perfectly straight. She shut her eyes as he misted it with hair spray.

"Have a good day," Hélène said as Yolande stepped out of her chair.

"She'll be having a good day all right," Marcel told Hélène. "She still has an appointment for a mineral bath and massage. The boyfriend's treat." Yolande straightened her shoulders. She liked people knowing she had a boyfriend. Especially one who was so generous.

"Sounds like an awfully nice guy." Hélène crossed her feet.

* * *

Hélène was applying more lipstick when Yolande walked into the changing room to drop her smock into a wicker basket. "You're a beauty," Hélène said matter-of-factly. "If I can give you a little advice …" She let her voice trail off.

"What is it?"

"You need to project more confidence. That boyfriend of yours won't be able to resist a confident woman. When you walk, you should sway your hips. Let me demonstrate." Hélène stepped along the floor and adjusted her hips so her butt stuck out. Yolande had to admit it made her look sexy.

Hélène whistled when Yolande tried it. "You're a quick learner," she said, and they both laughed.

* * *

Waves crashed and birds chirped from high in the trees. Usually, Yolande hated New Age music, but at the moment, she was getting into it. Even the patchouli incense wasn't making her nose itch. The problem was, how she was ever going to get up from the massage table and go back to real life?

Yolande tilted her neck a little to one side, then to the other. The masseuse had gotten all the kinks out.

There was a knock at the door. "Excuse me, Miss," a voice called. "Message for you. Your boyfriend phoned to say there'll be a cab waiting for you outside when you leave."

"Thank you," Yolande said, taking one last deep breath before she stepped down from the massage table. The sheet that had been covering her fell to the floor.

If only she could stay as calm and happy as she felt right now. Yolande couldn't wait to thank Etienne for his special treat.

But when Yolande stepped up to the cab, Etienne wasn't in the back seat. Someone else was.

For a second, Yolande thought she'd gotten into

the wrong cab. Then a voice came purring from the back seat. "Come right in, Tiffany." It was Hélène.

When Yolande looked over at the cab driver, she shivered. He was the same guy who'd driven Etienne and her to Josh's condo the other night. How was that for a weird coincidence?

Chapter 14

"Where's Etienne?" Yolande caught a glimpse of herself in the car's side mirror. Right now, not even perfect hair could cheer her up. She felt a shooting pain at the base of her neck. So much for the massage.

"Etienne's been called in to work. He asked us to come for you." Hélène's voice was less friendly than it had been at the spa. Now it had a sharper, bossier edge. "That's Desmond," she said, lifting her chin toward the driver.

Desmond nodded into the rear-view mirror. If he recognized Yolande, he didn't let on.

"Where are we going?" Yolande sounded bolder than she felt.

"For a little drive," Hélène said, patting Yolande's knee as if she was a little girl who'd fallen and scraped it on the sidewalk.

They were getting on the Decarie Expressway in the direction of downtown. "Now that we have a little more time, I can explain the rules of the game."

"What game?" Yolande shrugged her shoulders. Hélène had a weird way of speaking in riddles.

When Hélène laughed, little creases formed around her eyes. "The game. You're on the game now, Tiffany. Haven't you figured that out yet?"

Yolande pulled her jean jacket tightly over her shoulders. She had no idea what Hélène was talking about, but whatever it was didn't sound like Snakes and Ladders. "Does it have … something to do with … Etienne?" His name caught in her throat.

"Aren't you clever?" When Hélène smiled, Yolande could see all her teeth. "He picked you."

"I know he did," Yolande said, beginning to feel a little more confident. At least, Hélène seemed to understand how Etienne felt about her.

Hélène kept talking, paying no attention to Yolande's remark. "I suppose he told you all about his mama and the dead sister," she said.

Yolande nodded. "Of course he did. Etienne's been through so much."

"He sure has — and now he uses it to get what he wants. Etienne can spot girls like you a mile away. Girls who like pretty things, who like attention. Girls who miss their daddies. Sometimes they're girls like me: girls whose daddies got a little too friendly."

Yolande's eyes widened. Was Hélène saying she'd been molested by her father? No wonder she seemed so hard.

"None of that matters anymore," Hélène said, waving her hand in the air as if she could simply brush away the memory. "This is the way it is: Etienne's the boss. You're part of the stable. I'm his bottom bitch."

"His what?" What woman would call herself a bitch? And make it sound like it was something to be proud of?

"His bottom bitch," Hélène repeated, looking into Yolande's eyes as if she were challenging her. "I've been with him since he came from Haiti."

Hélène's gold bangles jingled on her wrist. Had they been a gift from Etienne, too? "You went out with Etienne?"

When Hélène spoke again, her voice was icy. "We're still going out." Yolande's mouth fell open and her chest started to hurt. For a second, she felt like she couldn't breathe, as if the air was trapped in her lungs. She wanted to say that none of this made any sense, that she was Etienne's girlfriend, but no words came out.

"He has other girls like you in the stable," Hélène continued, "but he always comes back to me." She lifted her head as she spoke so her long neck seemed even longer, reminding Yolande of a prize mare on race day.

"I don't want to be part of a stable," Yolande said, raising her voice. The car was air conditioned, but she felt droplets of sweat beginning to form at her temples and behind her knees. She looked up into the rearview mirror, hoping to catch

Desmond's eye, but he was staring out at the road. Yolande could tell he wasn't going to help her.

"You don't have a choice." Hélène rubbed her hands together. "You'll go out with whatever guy Etienne tells you to. Etienne collects the cash. You get something to cover your expenses. Clothing, shoes, hair, nails. It's important that you look pretty. Your life goes on as usual — summer camp, then back to school after Labour Day."

"You can have a drink now and then, but no drugs. Clients don't like girls who are strung out. Everything's cool as long as you don't tell anyone you're on the game — not even that little pal of yours."

"I can't have sex with a stranger," Yolande whispered. Her legs and arms felt heavy, as if she was in a dream she couldn't wake up from.

"You already did." Now Hélène's voice sounded tired, as if she'd said all this many times before and having to say it again bored her. "Rich Taylor was a stranger. So were those two at the party in Old Montreal. Technically, I suppose Josh last night wasn't a stranger since you'd done him before."

Yolande felt a wave of shame wash over her as she remembered the VIP room. How did Hélène know all that? "Those were mistakes," Yolande whispered, wiping the sweat from her upper lip.

"We don't make mistakes," Hélène said. "Our mistakes make us. And those mistakes of yours made you a whore."

Yolande made a choking noise.

"Don't get so upset. We're all whores. But only some of us get paid."

They had exited the highway and Desmond was slowing down. Yolande reached for the door handle. She had to get out of the car. Then her eyes met Desmond's in the rear-view mirror. He didn't say a word, but his eyes told her no. Absolutely not. Or else. Yolande dropped her hands back onto her lap.

The car was winding through the busy streets of Chinatown and up St-Laurent Boulevard. This was, Yolande knew, the worst neighbourhood in Montreal. They passed a dilapidated movie theatre that showed X-rated movies, and a cabaret with a huge billboard offering five-dollar lap dances.

At the stoplight, Yolande spotted a woman wearing a skin-tight leopard miniskirt and vinyl boots that reached to her thighs. Suddenly, the woman turned and peered into the cab. From behind, she looked like a teenager, but now Yolande realized she was probably in her forties. Her mom's age. Her haggard face was just feet from Yolande's. Yolande cringed, her shoulders hunching together so she seemed to take up less room in the back seat.

"You don't want to end up like her, do you?" Hélène asked. "Working the corners, looking for johns."

Yolande didn't say a word.

"Well, would you?"

"No, I wouldn't," Yolande said flatly, realizing

the only way to get Hélène to stop taunting her was to say something.

As the car headed north, Yolande turned around to take another look at the prostitute. A car had stopped at the corner and she was leaning over the driver's window. Making a deal. Yolande looked away.

"Etienne really likes you," Hélène said. Her voice was soft again, but now Yolande understood that Hélène's soft voice was just a cover for the hardness inside her. "He knows how to take care of a woman."

"He loves me," Yolande said, using the words like a shield — and trying desperately to make herself believe they were true. But somehow, even to her own ears, the words sounded hollow. If Etienne loved her, why would he want her to be part of some stable? And how could he still be seeing Hélène? How could any of it be true?

"Of course he does." This time, when Hélène reached over to pat Yolande's knee, Yolande moved away. "Don't be mad," Hélène whispered. "You're going to need me. I look out for the girls in Etienne's stable."

"How many are there?" Yolande asked, without turning to look at Hélène. It was a terrible question, but Yolande needed to know.

"Six — including you."

Yolande took a deep breath. "When does he see them all?" she asked, dropping her eyes to the vinyl mats on the floor of the car.

The question made Hélène laugh. "Etienne's a busy man. He doesn't get much sleep."

They were circling back toward downtown. Yolande knew she should be thinking about what Hélène had just told her, but she couldn't. It was too big — like a dark pit she didn't want to go into. If she ventured in, she might never find her way out.

Yolande tried to focus on the interior of the cab. The meter wasn't running. Then she looked at the photograph of Desmond hanging over the spot where his seat belt came out of the wall. It was an old black-and-white picture with frayed edges.

Desmond pulled up in front of the Royal Regency Hotel. Then he got out and walked around to open Yolande's door. When she looked at him, his expression was blank.

Hélène took a swipe card from the pocket of her purse. "Room 904," she told Yolande. "Your date's expecting you."

"904? That's Richie Taylor's room, isn't it?" The thought of Richie's suite and the way he'd admired her skin made Yolande feel a little better.

"It's not Richie's room. It's Etienne's," Hélène said, as if she were a teacher explaining something to a student who didn't get it.

"How come Etienne's got a room here?" Yolande asked, but she'd already begun to figure out the answer. That night with Richie hadn't just happened; Etienne had arranged it. Then Yolande remembered how he'd left the loft party without looking back at her. Had he planned all along to leave her with Josh and Tony? For a moment, Yolande felt her stomach lurch.

"Listen, Tiffany," Hélène said, watching Yolande's face. "You want to play with the big kids, don't you? Well then, you have to act like a big kid. Now be a good girl and go upstairs. Desmond and I'll be here waiting when you're done."

Yolande bit her lip. Then she took the swipe card.

Chapter 15

"I'm not some horse," Yolande said when Etienne opened the door to his apartment. The words had been going through her head all morning. When Etienne didn't answer his pager, Yolande decided she'd wait until her mother left for *satsang* and then go straight to his apartment.

"What're you talkin' about, Tiffany?" Etienne rubbed the sleep from his eyes. He was wearing grey boxers and his white tank top.

"Hélène told me about the —" Yolande's voice cracked when she tried to say the word "stable."

"Calm down, will you? If you keep carrying on like this, you'll wake up all the neighbours," Etienne said as he took hold of her wrists and pulled her inside.

"Is anyone else here?" Yolande scanned the apartment for signs of another visitor. Another woman. Shoes, a purse … but there was nothing.

"There's no one else here, silly," Etienne said,

tweaking the end of Yolande's nose and leaning in for a kiss.

Yolande turned her face away. "Hélène says you have lots of other girls. In your stable." This time she managed to get the word out.

"Hélène exaggerates. C'mon baby, I'm tired. Let's me and you go back to bed."

"I don't wanna go back to bed with you. I wanna talk." When Yolande stomped her foot, the corners of Etienne's lips curled up into a smile. She wanted him to take her seriously, but right now, he seemed more amused than upset.

"We'll talk later. I promise." This time, she let him kiss her. She inhaled his familiar scent as he pulled her onto the bed. The sheets were still warm.

* * *

"You're the best there is, baby," Etienne purred into her ear. His arms were around her, and they were facing each other. They'd kicked off the sheets so only their feet and ankles were still covered. The morning sun streamed in through the window. Overhead, the fan made a gentle hum.

"Are you sure? Better even than Hélène?" Yolande wished she hadn't needed to ask.

When Etienne laughed, Yolande felt her whole body — even her toes — relax. "Better than anybody," he assured her.

Yolande sighed. Despite everything that had happened, Etienne still knew how to make her feel good. She wrapped her arms around his neck, thinking how she couldn't seem to resist him. She wished she could — but she couldn't. She closed her eyes and tried to pretend this moment would last forever.

The steady sound of Etienne's breathing made Yolande feel calm and safe. But there were things she and Etienne still needed to straighten out. "I don't want to fool around with anyone else ever aga—" she whispered.

"I know how you feel, Tiffany," Etienne said, rocking her in his arms. "But you said you wanted to help me."

"I do. But I don't want to have — you know — sex … with strangers. Doing that kind of stuff means too much to me." She looked into his eyes, sure that would make him understand how she felt. "I only want to do it with you." Yolande took a deep breath. "And I only want you to do it with me."

Etienne made a snorting sound. "You have to," he said as he combed his fingers through her hair.

Yolande let go of Etienne. "I have to what?"

"You have to do it again. For me."

That was exactly what she'd been afraid he'd say. Afraid all night. "I won't. I can't." Yolande covered her face with her hands.

Then without saying anything, she got up from the bed and pulled on her jeans and T-shirt. She could hear the padding sounds Etienne made as he followed her into the living room. But Yolande didn't turn around to look at him.

"I have something to show you that might make you change your mind."

"What are you talking about?" Yolande had sat down on a chair to put on her shoes, but suddenly it seemed as if everything around her, including Etienne, was on an odd angle.

Etienne reached for the remote control on the glass coffee table and hit the play button. "If you don't, I'll have to send a copy of this tape to your mom — and to all her friends at the meditation centre."

Yolande winced when she saw the first image. Etienne's long, broad back, her pale body beneath his, her mouth open. "Turn it off!" she shouted.

"Why should I? I like watching me and you in action!"

Yolande grabbed the remote from Etienne's hand. "Who shot it?" she asked as the screen turned black. "Was someone else here when we were making love?"

"Don't worry!" Etienne said, laughing. "I rigged up my camcorder in one of the shelves over my bed. Hey, I never expected a girl as hot as you to be shy."

"Throw it out!" Yolande insisted, grabbing a pillow from Etienne's couch and pressing it to her chest.

Etienne just kept laughing. "Even if I did, I've got another copy stashed away. For safekeeping."

Then Etienne's eyes softened. His voice was gentle when he spoke again. "I told you how whatever you do with other guys won't mean anything. All that counts is us. Me and you, Tiffany."

And because she wanted to believe him, Yolande stopped arguing.

Chapter 16

Gabrielle checked her watch. Yolande looked up at the clock and bit her lip.

It was already 3:10 p.m. and they were each stuck with one camper whose parents hadn't yet shown up. The temperature had soared to the high twenties and the fan in the lobby of the Y wasn't doing much except stir the warm air. Yolande glanced out at the street. Desmond would be there soon.

"My mommy's always on time," Gabrielle's camper said. He had his hands in the pockets of his grass-stained overalls, and he sounded worried.

Gabrielle put her arms around him. "I'm sure she's on her way, Jacky."

"My mom's always late," Yolande's camper, a girl with blonde pigtails, said.

"Just my luck," Yolande muttered under her breath.

"Should we phone their parents?" Gabrielle asked Yolande. It was the first complete sentence either of the girls had said to each other all day.

"I guess," Yolande said, without looking at Gabrielle.

"I'll go phone."

Yolande nodded.

"Hey, look! Both our moms are here!" Jacky grabbed his backpack from the floor and the two kids hurried out to the sidewalk.

"Wanna walk home together?" Gabrielle asked.

"I've got other plans," Yolande said as Desmond's cab pulled up to the curb.

Gabrielle followed Yolande out of the building. "So who's that guy?"

"Nobody you know."

"I don't know *you* anymore," Gabrielle said to Yolande's back.

Yolande spun around. "Why can't you mind your own business?" The second she said the words, Yolande began to regret them. She didn't mean to keep pushing Gabrielle away. If only she and Gabs could just go back to simpler times, when all they had to worry about was fashion magazines and math assignments.

But there was nothing to do about it because this time, it was Gabrielle who turned her back and rushed down the street.

Besides, Desmond was waiting.

* * *

Yolande wished there'd been time to shower. She felt dirty. Grimy, even. Not just because she'd spent the afternoon out on the playing field with her campers. More because of what she was about to do. Only it was the kind of dirty that wouldn't wash away in the shower.

She wished there was someone she could talk to. In a way, it was just as well she and Gabrielle were fighting. There was no way Gabs could handle any of this.

As Yolande slid into the cab, an image from the video Etienne had taken popped into her head. She tried to push it away, but the image kept reappearing. One thing was for sure: her mom would die if she ever saw the video. And no amount of yoga or meditation could revive her.

"Do you ever say anything?" she asked Desmond.

Desmond looked into the rear-view mirror and met her eyes. "Hardly ever."

"Well that's two words. Are you taking me to the Royal?"

"Not today."

"Why not?"

Desmond shrugged.

"So where are we going?"

"You'll see."

"You're not much fun."

"Just doing my job." Desmond's eyes were back on the road.

Yolande didn't say a word. Was that what she was doing, too? The thought made her feel sad. And hopeless.

Desmond pulled into a parking lot near the Bell Centre. "Your date's waiting in that car," he said, nodding toward a black sedan. Its motor was running. "Name's Henry."

Yolande took a deep breath as Desmond helped her out of the back seat. "I won't be far away," he whispered, without looking at her. His gaze was fixed straight ahead, as if he was still in the car, concentrating on the road.

* * *

She'd seen Henry at the The Basement. Dark hair parted down the middle. Why didn't someone do him a favour and tell him to get a decent haircut?

"Thought we'd go for a spin," Henry said, tapping the steering wheel with one finger.

"Can you believe this heat wave?" Yolande asked, trying to make conversation. After a few weeks on the game, she'd learned that some guys were more interested in conversation than anything else. "Their wives don't listen to them," Hélène had explained. "A woman who listens — now that's as big a turn-on as great tits or a great ass."

"I built my business from scratch," Henry said, as they drove out of the parking lot. "Now I've got eleven full-time employees."

Yolande nodded, pretending to be interested as Henry described his contracting company. When someone wanted to renovate a house, he'd hook them up with plumbers, electricians, carpenters … whatever. "I'm a middleman. I keep my hands clean," he said, inspecting his pale fingers as they gripped the steering wheel. "I make the connections."

"I guess summer's a busy time for you," Yolande said. As she smiled at Henry, she couldn't help wishing she was someplace else. Hanging out with Etienne ... or sitting on her pale pink carpet, reading *Cosmo* with Gabrielle. She'd been in such a hurry to grow up, but now that she was playing with the big kids, all Yolande wanted to do was go back to being a little kid again.

"You're right." Henry's hand grazed her knee when he reached to turn on the radio. He scanned the stations until he found one he liked. "Soft rock. That okay with you?"

"Sure," Yolande said, lying. In her opinion, soft rock was for old fogies. But she didn't think Henry would be into rap. "Where're we going?" she asked, suddenly realizing they were driving through an industrial neighbourhood she didn't recognize. Yolande turned to look behind her. A moving van blocked her view. Where was Desmond?

"I want to show you my office," Henry said, pulling into a small parking lot.

When he turned off the engine, Yolande undid her seat belt and reached for the door handle.

"No," Henry said, laying his hand over hers. His fingers felt cold and clammy. Yolande tried to smile. "I thought you wanted me to see your office."

"I do." Henry's voice was gruff. "But I want you to do something first."

Yolande thought he was going to kiss her. But he didn't. Instead, he reached behind her and pressed his fingertips against her right shoulder, pushing her down so her face was only an inch or two from his groin. He was wearing black dress pants.

Yolande's shoulder burned where his fingers dug in. She wanted to shake herself free, but she couldn't. He had her pinned to the seat.

She could tell Henry was excited. She shut her eyes tight. "Shouldn't we go —" she tried asking as she heard the scraping sound of Henry unzipping his pants.

He brought his hand to the back of her neck and pressed down even harder. Yolande understood what she was supposed to do. She reached into her bag for a condom.

As her lips parted, her eyes landed on the ashtray. It was overflowing with ashes and cigarette butts. At the back, Yolande spotted a wadded up piece of green gum. Had she been chewing gum when she got into the car? Strange the stuff you think about when you're doing something you don't want to do.

When Henry moaned, Yolande tried to imagine Etienne.

Chapter 17

They'd spent almost all night together. Just the two of them. Like Etienne had promised.

He'd brought her to the private health club he belonged to. They'd eaten shrimp salad and sipped cappuccinos at the bar by the swimming pool. Then they'd taken a jacuzzi together, the jets of water pulsing from behind their knees and at their shoulders. It was a real date — not the kind of creepy date Yolande was getting used to.

It was hard to stay angry with Etienne. He held her hand in the jacuzzi and kissed the side of her neck. When he looked into her eyes, Yolande still quivered inside. Despite everything.

"Gabs and I fought again," she admitted over the sound of the jacuzzi's motor. "I told her to mind her own business."

Etienne stroked her hand. Their fingers were wrinkled from the hot water. "You shouldn't get mad at Gabrielle, Tiffany. She needs you. And we need her."

Yolande bristled. "Need Gabrielle? For what —
part of your stable?" she asked, looking at Etienne
over the steaming bubbles.

"It's not that," he said. "Gabrielle's part of your
other life. And you've got to keep that life smooth
and uncomplicated. No fights, okay? I want you to
keep all that wild animal passion for me!"

"Okay," Yolande said, relaxing when he leaned
in to kiss her and run his fingers along the soft
skin on the inside of her thigh. Sometimes she
wished she could resist him. But she couldn't. She
just couldn't.

* * *

Etienne was right about her having another life. In
fact, as Yolande walked through the mall with her
mom, she decided she had three lives. One — the
best one, by far — when she and Etienne were
together; one when she was with a client; and one
when she was at home or at camp.

At the moment, it was taking everything
Yolande had not to explode at her mom, who'd
insisted she come to the mall to buy groceries at
the IGA. "If you ate more raw veggies, you'd
have more energy," her mom was saying. She'd
hooked her arm through Yolande's and Yolande
was too tired to pull away. The late nights were
catching up with her.

Yolande covered her mouth when she felt a
yawn coming on. "See what I mean," her mom

said, shaking her head. "We really have to increase your chi energy."

If there was one thing Yolande wasn't in the mood to talk about, it was chi energy. "What do you think of those shoes?" she asked. She'd stopped to point at a pair of blue, denim Mary Janes in the window at Aldo. They'd go perfectly with her jean skirt.

Thinking of her jean skirt reminded Yolande of the night she'd first met Etienne. It had been the happiest night in all her life. At the time, it had seemed that only good things were ahead. Now everything was different. Everything was complicated.

"Impractical," was her mom's verdict. She glanced down approvingly at her own Birkenstocks. "Imagine going for a walk in those flimsy denim things. Honestly, Yolande, sometimes I find it hard to believe we're related."

"Me, too," Yolande muttered under her breath.

"Is it time for new shoes?"

Yolande shivered. She remembered how, when she was little, her mom and dad used to ask her that question. Then the three of them would go to Kiddie Kobbler to pick out a new pair of shoes. Once, as a special treat, they'd bought her a pair of shiny, red cowboy boots. She could still remember the clopping sound they made when she wore them in the kitchen.

"Nah," Yolande said, crossing her arms and turning away from the store window. "I can use my money from camp for what I need."

Mrs. Owen looked at Yolande as if she were some exotic animal, like a Bengal tiger or a pygmy chimpanzee. "I'm glad you want to be independent. In fact, I noticed a new striped halter top in the laundry." Then Mrs. Owen slowed her pace as if she was gearing up to say something important. "I just hope you're shopping the sales."

Yolande chewed on her lip so she wouldn't smile. Sometimes, there were advantages to having a parent who was so out of it. Her mother knew as much about labels like Miss Sixty as Yolande know about chi energy.

"All right then," her mom said, "let's check out the natural foods counter at the IGA."

"All right, then!" Yolande said, mimicking her mom. Mrs. Owen smiled, oblivious to Yolande's sarcasm.

Two middle-aged men were sitting on a bench, chatting outside the Hallmark store. They fell silent as Yolande and her mother approached. Yolande knew they were checking her out. Usually, she'd have enjoyed the attention, but today, it irritated her. One of the men wore his hair parted down the middle like Henry.

In the distance, Yolande noticed a familiar head of dark frizzy hair. It was Gabrielle with her dad and Aggie. Yolande thought about saying hi, but then she remembered their last argument. Even if Etienne wanted her to keep this part of her life smooth and uncomplicated, even if she had been out of line by getting so upset, Yolande wasn't ready to forgive Gabrielle. Not yet, anyway.

"Hey, Mom," she said, leading her into the drugstore. "Don't we need toothpaste?" The fluorescent lighting made Yolande's head hurt.

"You know I prefer the toothpaste we get at the health food store. Fewer additives." Mrs. Owen gave Yolande an odd look.

But it was too late. Aggie had spotted them. She had pried her hand loose from her father's and was running down the shampoo aisle toward Yolande and her mother.

"Yo-yo!" she called out.

Gabrielle and her dad followed Aggie into the drugstore. "Nice to see you, Sheila," Gabrielle's dad said. Gabrielle shifted from one foot to the other, her eyes cast down to the white tile floor.

"We're making a barbecue tonight," Aggie announced. "We're going to the IGA for hamburger meat and marshmallows. Can you come for the barbecue?" she asked, looking up at Yolande with hopeful eyes.

"Um. I don't know." Yolande looked over at her mom.

"You're not serving hamburger and marshmallows on the same bun are you?" Mrs. Owen asked Gabrielle's dad.

That made Aggie giggle. "C'mon, Yo-yo. She can come, Dad, can't she?" Aggie turned from Yolande to her dad.

"Sure," he said. "You're welcome too, Sheila. If you're free."

Yolande watched as her mother twisted her wedding ring around her finger. "I wish I could," her mom said, "but I have a meditation workshop tonight. Of course, Yolande can go if she'd like to."

"Um. I don't think so. I think I'll stay home and eat tofu dogs with my mom. Tofu's really good for you," Yolande told Aggie.

Gabrielle looked up from the floor and rolled her eyes.

"Hey, aren't those Miss Sixty jeans?" Aggie called out, inspecting the label on the back pocket of Yolande's jeans. "Aren't they like two hundr—" Aggie cut herself off when she saw Yolande's glare.

Luckily, her mom was busy talking with Gabrielle and Aggie's dad. "Tofu dogs should work on the barbecue," she was saying. "Only you wouldn't want to grill them for too long."

Together they all headed for the IGA. "Do you mind not sticking to me like glue?" Gabrielle asked Aggie. "I need to talk to Yolande."

For a second, Aggie looked disappointed, but then she skipped down the vegetable aisle to join the two adults.

Gabrielle checked to make sure she and Yolande were alone. "Look, I'm really sorry I've been getting on your case. It's just — sometimes I feel like I don't know you anymore. The thing is, Yo-yo, I'm worried about you."

"You know, Gabs, maybe you worry too much. It's not like I'm miserable or anything. I'm with a great guy. An amazing guy." She let her voice wander off as if she really were thinking about how amazing Etienne was. "Did you ever think maybe you're just jealous?"

Gabrielle blushed so hard even her scalp turned red. "Okay, maybe," she said, speaking more slowly than usual. "I admit I sometimes wish I was going out with someone, too. Someone who'd make a big deal over me like Etienne does with you. But I still feel like something's wrong. You're always tired and in a bad mood and you never really listen anymore …"

Yolande took a box of breakfast cereal from one of the shelves. On it was a picture of a family seated at a round table. A mom and dad and two angelic looking children. She put the box back on the shelf. "I'm listening to you now, aren't I? And you'd better listen to me, Gabs. I'm changing, okay? Why can't you understand that?"

"I don't know. I just can't."

Gabrielle looked so small and sad that Yolande couldn't help reaching out and taking her hand. She suddenly remembered other times they'd held hands. On the first day of kindergarten. Waiting for the school bus on a wintry morning. At an audition for the grade 6 play.

Yolande didn't want to lose Etienne, but now she realized she didn't want to lose Gabrielle, either. Gabs was her connection to the past. To simpler times. To times when a game was just a game.

Besides, Etienne was right. She had to keep her

other life smooth and uncomplicated. "Look, Gabs, I want us to get along, too."

That was when Gabrielle noticed the line of small purple bruises on Yolande's right shoulder. There were four of them, all small, but with a familiar oval shape. Fingerprints.

Gabrielle covered her mouth with her hand. "Oh, God! Did he do that to you?"

Chapter 18

Yolande had insisted Gabrielle borrow the striped halter top for the concert. "I can't wear it, obviously," she'd said. She didn't want anyone else to notice the bruises. Though they'd faded from purple to yellow, they were still visible, like a sprinkling of pale buttercups on one shoulder. Of course, there was another fingerprint Gabrielle hadn't noticed. It was under Yolande's armpit, where Henry's thumb had dug in.

Yolande had laughed when Gabrielle had asked about the bruises. "Maybe Etienne was holding me too tight when we were … you know …" she'd said. But she'd had a feeling Gabrielle didn't believe her.

Now Yolande's pale eyes glowed in the dimness of the Bell Centre. They had front-row seats for Sweet Innocence. Richie Taylor had given Etienne two tickets for Yolande and she'd invited Gabrielle as her guest. Even if they'd lined up all night, they'd never have been able to get such great seats. Even better, they were invited backstage after the concert.

Yolande closed her eyes when the band began to play. She let herself escape into the music — the thrumming of the guitar, the beat of the drums — so that for a few minutes, at least, she could forget the game. Was this why people loved music and movies and books? So they could escape from the rest of their lives?

After the opening set, when Richie danced across the stage and tipped his cowboy hat at her, Yolande screamed.

Even Gabrielle, who wasn't the type to be starstruck, was impressed. "I can't believe he came right over," she shouted, loud enough so Yolande would hear her over the band.

"I know," Yolande said, without taking her eyes off the stage. "He's cute, isn't he?"

"Really cute," Gabrielle agreed.

"How old do you think he is?"

"It's hard to tell. But he was a star when our parents were teenagers, so he's got to be in his late forties. Maybe even early fifties."

"Do you really think he's that old?" said Yolande.

"Check out the grey chest hair," Gabrielle said.

The Bell Centre went quiet as Richie, illuminated by a giant yellow spotlight, walked to centre stage. Tucking his hands into his back pockets, he leaned into the microphone as if he was about to kiss it. "Bonsoir, Montréal," he said in a gravelly voice, taking one hand from his pocket and reaching for a towel to wipe the sweat from his forehead. "We've got a special treat for you tonight."

Richie grinned as the crowd broke into noisy cheers. "We're gonna perform our new song, 'Skin Like Silk.' This is our first time playing it in public."

The Bell Centre went wild. "Yeah!" the audience roared and suddenly the concert hall was flickering with tiny yellow lights. People were using their lighters like candles.

"She's got skin like silk," the band members sang into their microphones. Their voices grew louder as the song went on. "She's got hair like flax. But it ain't what you think. I ain't just another john. She's on the game …"

It was the kind of song that made you want to join in. Yolande nodded her head to the beat.

Gabrielle mouthed the words, then she started singing out loud with the rest of the audience. "Skin like silk …"

Just then, Richie looked directly at Yolande. Then he did something even more unexpected. He winked. "I ain't just …" he sang.

"Oh, my God," Gabrielle's voice was sharp. Then she said the rest of the line out loud, without singing it this time: "another john." Her back and shoulders stiffened.

She nudged Yolande. "It's about you, isn't it?"

Yolande paid no attention to Gabrielle. It was as if she was under the song's spell.

"It's you! You're on the game!" Gabrielle hissed, so loudly the man sitting next to them turned around and said, "Shh!" raising one finger to his lips like a cross.

"It's just a song," Yolande said when the band stopped playing and the explosion of cheering and clapping was over.

"It's not just a song," Gabrielle insisted. "It's about a girl with silky skin and hair like flax. Like you." Gabrielle's hands were shaking. "Only she's a whore."

"You know something, Gabs? You're out of your mind!"

"The presents. The shoes. The jewelry. The late nights. Etienne. Oh, God, the marks on your shoulder. It's all starting to make sense!"

As long as Gabrielle didn't know about the game, Yolande could at least pretend her life was still normal. But how had Gabrielle figured it out? "It's not true," Yolande insisted, her voice rising.

"He's so adorable!" a female voice shouted from the far end of their row. Both girls turned in the direction of the voice. It belonged to a woman carrying a single red rose wrapped in cellophane. The woman next to her was holding a rose, too. Both of them were attractive, but in a showy way, with big, blow-dried hair and way too much eyeshadow.

"Wanna bet they're invited backstage, too?" Gabrielle asked.

* * *

The security guard waved Yolande and Gabrielle through when he saw their backstage passes. There was nothing glamorous about backstage. Basically, it was a mess of wires and lights. A spot on the floor had been turned into a makeshift bar. Bottles of beer glistened inside a plastic cooler; liquor and wine bottles were piled haphazardly inside a cardboard crate.

Gabrielle was right about the two women with the roses. They were backstage, perched on either side of Richie Taylor.

"Tiffany!" Richie called out when Yolande walked in. She could feel the rose women staring at her.

Yolande let her lips brush Richie's, then she turned to Gabrielle. "This is my friend … Sasha."

"My name's not —" A sharp look from Yolande stopped Gabrielle in mid-sentence.

"Great to meet you, Sasha." Richie reached for Gabrielle's hand.

"The concert was amazing," Yolande said.

A roadie wearing jeans and a torn T-shirt slapped Richie on the shoulder. "Phone call for you, man," he said. Lowering his voice, he added, "from home."

"Gimme five minutes," Richie told Yolande as he headed for the dressing room.

"I'm Heather," said one of the rose women. "This here's Ginger," she added, introducing her

119

friend. "Anyone for a beer?" Heather bent down to reach into the cooler. The pink top she was wearing inched up her back.

Gabrielle nudged Yolande again. "Check out the tattoo, " she whispered, eyeing Heather's sun-tanned back.

There was no mistaking the letters E. G.

"She works for him, too, doesn't she?" It was a question, but the way it came out — matter-of-factly and calmly — made Yolande realize she couldn't go on fooling her friend. Or herself.

Chapter 19

The roadie's name was Brian. He'd been busy
mixing tequila, Triple Sec, and lime juice in a
plastic jug. Now he flipped a glass over and
pressed it into a plate of coarse salt. "These margaritas are gonna taste like they do in Tijuana."

The other band members had joined the party
now, too. One had pulled off his T-shirt, which
was drenched in sweat, and was walking around
bare chested. Another was still humming "Skin
Like Silk," tapping his fingers to the song's beat.
"They totally loved that tune." he said to no one in
particular.

Heather and Ginger seemed to know everyone.
"How'd your gig in Vancouver go?" Ginger asked
the drummer, whose hair was as long and blonde
as Yolande's.

"It went great, but it ain't Montreal," the drummer told Ginger. "How come all the really
gorgeous women live in this city?"

Ginger laughed.

"Do you really think so?" Heather asked, and the drummer said he did.

When he tapped his knee, Ginger went to sit on his lap like a pet cat.

Brian refilled Yolande's glass.

Gabrielle sipped at her margarita, surveying her surroundings over the edge of her glass. "So you know Etienne?" Gabrielle was talking to Heather, but for a second, her eyes met Yolande's.

Heather's lips tightened when she smiled.

At the mention of Etienne's name, Ginger turned away from the drummer and stared at Gabrielle.

"Everyone knows Etienne," Heather said, flicking a tight, blonde ringlet from her face. "Ginger and I are —" here she dropped her voice, "part of the stable. But we're getting a little long in the tooth for Etienne's clients."

"Long in the tooth?" Gabrielle asked.

"You know — old. A few wrinkles … a little flab," she said, patting her belly. "Etienne's clients like their girls young and firm — and inexperienced. So they can tell them what to do. Kind of like the two of you."

Yolande's mind flashed back to what had happened in Henry's car. Heather was right. Henry had told her exactly what he wanted her to do. And she hadn't had the courage to object.

Gabrielle nearly toppled off her stool. "I'm not part of any stable," she said, but Heather wasn't listening.

Richie had walked back into the room. He'd changed from his jeans and T-shirt into a red, satin smoking jacket. Little tufts of curly grey hair peeked out at his chest. His feet were bare and the toenail on his big toe was long and gnarled looking. "I see you're getting acquainted," he said, smiling his lopsided smile. "Heather and Ginger are … old friends," he told Yolande and Gabrielle.

"That's what they've been telling us." Yolande forced herself to smile up at Richie.

Richie pulled over a stool and threw his arm around her waist. "It's great to see you again, baby," he whispered into her ear, but loudly enough for the others to hear.

The drummer was passing around cans of beer. "Nothing like a cold Canadian beer on a hot night — especially when there are hot women around," he said.

Gabrielle blushed.

Ginger laughed.

"Hey guys, I brought some pot." Heather reached into her purse and pulled out a baggie filled with dry, brown leaves.

"I just happen to have some rolling paper," the drummer said, digging into his front pocket.

"You roll, Richie." Heather passed Richie the marijuana and the drummer handed him the packet of rolling papers.

"We need some music. This is a party, isn't it?" Richie opened the baggie and lifted it up to his nose.

Jimmy got up to put on a CD — a compilation of the band's greatest hits.

Richie's fingers worked as deftly as a machine. He lit the joint, took a deep drag, and held his breath until his cheeks puffed up. Then he leaned over as if he was about to kiss Yolande, but instead he blew the smoke into her mouth. Then he passed the joint to Heather.

Suddenly, there was a loud banging at the backstage door. "See who it is, Brian," Richie said.

The drummer took a quick puff, then held the joint down to hide it from the man at the door.

"What's going on in here?" a gruff voice asked.

"Take it easy, James," Richie called out. "We're having ourselves a little party is all."

The drummer's shoulders relaxed as he passed the joint to Ginger.

Yolande could tell from his grey pinstripe suit that James wasn't a musician. "Listen, Richie," he said, clapping his hands together, "there's a camera crew coming to interview you in ten minutes. I want you to clear these," he stopped to find the right word, "ladies — out of here."

"Ever heard the expression, 'All work and no play makes Jack a dull boy'? You trying to turn me into a dull boy, James?" Richie asked.

James ignored the question. He handed Richie a Styrofoam cup filled with mud-coloured coffee. "Drink up. I'd rather have you smelling of coffee than margaritas and pot."

Richie laughed. "This here's James," he told

Yolande and Gabrielle. "My handler."

"Sometimes I feel more like your babysitter," James muttered as he took the joint from Ginger's lips and squashed it in an ashtray. Then he waved his arms in the air to disperse the smoke. "Is there a window we can open in here?"

Heather and Ginger stood up to go. "If you don't need me for the interview, man," the drummer told Richie, "I'm going to see these lovely ladies home."

"How about we meet back at the Royal, Tiffany?" Richie asked. "Sasha, you come, too. You can keep Brian over here company." Richie slapped Brian on the back. "How's that sound, man?"

"Sounds good," Brian said, grinning shyly at Gabrielle.

Gabrielle blushed. "I — I don't think —" she stammered.

Yolande turned to Gabrielle. The colour had drained from her skin and one of her knees was shaking. For the first time, Yolande realized that maybe she and Gabrielle weren't so different after all. In spite of all of Gabs's high and mighty opinions, even a girl like her — a girl who followed all the rules — could get dragged into the game.

Yolande nodded at Gabrielle. Then she tapped Richie's elbow. "I'll meet you at the Royal," she told him. "But Sasha has to go straight home."

* * *

Desmond didn't say anything when Yolande told him they were taking Gabrielle back to NDG. "After that, you can drop me at the Royal," she added.

"Are you sure you'll be all right?" Gabrielle asked Yolande when the cab stopped at her corner.

"I'm a big girl." Then Yolande lifted one finger to her mouth. She'd protected Gabrielle. In return, Gabrielle would have to promise not to tell anyone Yolande's secret.

Gabrielle nodded. "Thanks for looking after me," she said as she stepped out of the cab.

When Desmond made a U-turn, the two girls looked at each other. It seemed like Gabrielle was about to wave, but then her hand dropped back to her side. It was as if her worry and fear had drained her energy. As the cab drove off into the darkness, Yolande closed her eyes. She'd never felt further away from her friend.

* * *

Richie was emerging from a long, white limousine just as Yolande got out of the cab. He stretched out his arms when he saw her.

That was when the lights started flashing. Big white lights that came out of the air like lightning. Yolande covered her eyes to protect them from the glare. A photographer was crouched by the car, his camera pointing at Yolande and Richie like a gun.

"You idiot! Get away from her! Now!" a voice boomed. It was James.

But it was too late. The photographer had already snapped several shots of the two of them outside the hotel.

"How old are you, miss?" a woman's voice asked.

Someone tugged at Yolande's arm. Seconds later, she was back in the cab and Desmond was peeling out of the driveway. "Holy shit!" he muttered as the tires squealed on the pavement.

Chapter 20

Is it ever dead around here. The thought made Yolande laugh, though she hadn't meant it as a joke.

Meeting at Mount Royal Cemetery had been Etienne's idea. "Me and you need to keep a low profile," he'd told her when she suggested they get together at the Second Cup on Monkland. "Besides," he'd added, "the cemetery is like a park. Only quieter. And more romantic."

Romance was the last thing on Yolande's mind. As she walked through the iron cemetery gates, she wondered if she even believed in romance anymore. All she really believed in lately was people using each other.

Even so, she'd agreed to meet Etienne. Without expecting to, Yolande whispered his name as she walked along the gravel path. She couldn't help picturing his broad shoulders, his smooth brown skin, the soft hair along his forearms and on his legs. For a moment, she felt a pang of longing for the way things were when she'd first fallen in love with him. If only there were some way of going back to that time.

The plastic shopping bag Yolande was carrying bumped against her knee. She'd stopped at the mall on the way and bought the denim Mary Janes. Buying them had given her a rush, but the feeling hadn't lasted. They were just another pair of shoes. Even the Tiffany bracelet dangling from her wrist didn't give her much pleasure anymore. It was all just stuff.

Yolande read the inscriptions on the tombstones she passed. Roland Leblanc, 1841–1902, always in our hearts. Edgar Dupuis, 1852–1911, greatly missed. Abigail Ellis, 1820–1897, beloved wife and mother. What would they write on her tombstone one day? Wife and mother? Not too likely.

A pair of fat robins chirped on a nearby branch. Their red bellies looked as round and full as pincushions. There were probably plenty of worms in these parts.

Yolande heard Etienne before she saw him. "Relax, man! I'm about to take care of it," he was saying into his cellphone.

It sounded like a dog was barking on the other end.

Etienne nodded when he saw her, but he didn't get off the phone. "Listen, James," he said in a tense voice, "I'm looking into it. I said I'd get back to you by seven. Now's not a very good time." Then he hung up.

Etienne opened his arms to hug Yolande. For a second, he looked like one of the stone angels on a nearby grave. Yolande shuddered. "Come on, Tiffany, let me hug you."

But Yolande couldn't relax in Etienne's arms. Her body felt tense, jumpy. "Something's wrong, isn't it?" Yolande's voice caught in her throat.

"Uh-huh. Like I told you on the phone this morning, you and me need to keep a low profile." Etienne paused, then dropped his voice as if he didn't even want the ghosts to hear what he was about to say. "I don't like to think about what would happen if the cops find out about us."

"What would happen?"

"You're underage, Tiffany. They can throw me in jail for that."

Yolande nearly forgot to breathe. "They can't do that. We love each other."

"Of course we do." Etienne brushed her forehead with his palm.

The anger and sadness Yolande had been feeling lately seemed, suddenly, to disappear. Now all Yolande felt was afraid. A cold, clammy fear that crept through her whole body. What would she do without him? How could she survive without Etienne as her boyfriend?

"They couldn't break us up!" She looked into Etienne's eyes. "Nothing could. Right?"

Etienne squeezed her hand again. "Right."

"Look," Yolande said. She was speaking quickly now. "Gabs knows about the game. I couldn't help it. She figured it out at the backstage party for Sweet Innocence."

Etienne slid one finger back and forth along the skin between his nose and lips. "Will she tell?"

"No," Yolande said, remembering how terrified Gabrielle had looked last night when she got out of the cab.

"Wanna go for a walk?" Etienne extended his hand.

"Nah. I'm too tired. Let's just sit," Yolande gestured toward a white marble bench by a nearby grave.

Etienne wrapped one arm around her when they sat down. "Things have been pretty tough lately, haven't they?"

Yolande would have liked to cry, but she couldn't. It was as if the tears were stuck in her throat and behind her eyes. Which only made her want to cry more.

"Things'll get better soon. I promise."

Yolande took a deep breath and turned toward Etienne. "You do?" She wanted so much to believe him.

"I do," Etienne said, kissing her lightly on the lips.

Yolande straightened her back. "Did Desmond tell you about the photographer?"

Etienne nodded.

"Where was the photographer from?"

"One of the fan magazines. *Meddler*, I think. There was a reporter, too. I heard she was asking

131

a lot of questions at the hotel after you left."

"Uh-oh," Yolande said, suddenly remembering the woman who'd asked her age. "So now what?"

"James is pretty upset. He's Richie's handler. He keeps phoning," Etienne said, eyeing his pager.

"I met him. He seemed kinda stressed out."

"Stressed out's not the right word. He's worried Richie's wife'll go ballistic if she finds out about you."

"Richie's married?" Yolande raised her eyebrows.

"They're all married." Etienne shrugged his shoulders. He didn't seem to notice when Yolande flinched. "This one's the third wife. She doesn't know he fools around on her. What's even worse is her daddy owns the record label. That's another reason why you need to lie low for a few days."

"What do you mean?"

"I mean no after-hours clubs. No dates. And no conversations with strangers. You got that?"

"Does that mean I'm grounded?" Yolande asked with a nervous giggle. She'd miss the after-hours clubs, but she was relieved about the dates. The game was starting to get to her, wearing her down.

"Basically."

"Can I still see you?" Yolande slid her knee alongside Etienne's. He wasn't perfect — in fact, she knew now that he was far from it — but she still wanted to be with him. No matter what. Besides, wasn't that what love really was? Finding out the truth about someone — all their flaws and secrets — and still being able to love them?

"That wouldn't be a very good idea."

Yolande pouted. "Come on! Can't I still come to your apartment?"

"No, you can't. Not for now. Look, I'll call you in a few days and we'll take things from there. In the meantime, just do what you did before you met me. Go to camp, hang out with your pal, that kind of stuff."

Yolande was quiet for a moment. "What's weird is," she said, looking up at the clouds, "I can't remember what I did before I met you."

* * *

"I feel like I'm under house arrest. Can you come over?"

"Dad!" Yolande could hear Gabrielle shouting to her father, which meant he was probably in the basement, watching sports. "Can I go over to Yo-yo's?" Yolande moved the receiver away from her face.

"Okay," Gabrielle said, "I'm on my way."

"Did you get the new *Cosmo?*"

"It didn't come yet. How about I pick up a *Glamour* magazine on my way?"

* * *

Gabrielle's face was flushed when she turned up at Yolande's door. "Is your mom home?" she asked, kicking off her sneakers in the front hallway.

"What? You're not gonna line them up neatly?" Yolande said, pointing to the floor. One sneaker, its laces still tied together in a fat loop, was upside down; the other one lay sprawled in the middle of the hallway, waiting for someone to trip over it.

"Is she home?" Gabrielle asked again.

"She's at the health food store. She was so excited when I said you were staying for supper, she went out to get ingredients for carrot shakes."

"That sounds gross."

"My opinion exactly."

"Guess who I saw at Multi-Mags?" Gabrielle said as she followed Yolande upstairs.

"The twins?"

"Nope."

"Madame Leroux?"

"Nope."

"Etienne?"

"No way!"

"So who'd you see?"

"You!"

"Me? What are you talking about? I've been here all day losing my mind."

"You! You're on the cover of *Meddler*. You and Richie Taylor. You look great, by the way." Gabrielle took out the *Glamour* magazine she'd brought along, opening it to the page in the middle where the staples were. A tabloid, folded in half, fell out and landed at Yolande's feet.

"Shit!" Yolande said, reaching for it. "Lemme see."

"I told you you look great." Gabrielle watched as Yolande examined the grainy photo on the cover. "Let's just hope your mom doesn't read *Meddler*."

"Or Richie's wife."

"Richie has a wife?"

"They all do," Yolande said.

"That's disgusting. Don't you feel bad for her?"

"Don't go getting all judgmental again, Gabs. I didn't know he was married. It's not like he wears a ring."

"Your mom'll kill you if she finds out."

"Murder is against her religion. Remember James, the handler? He's worried Richie's wife'll go ballistic. Plus her dad's in the music business."

"That's it!" Gabrielle sounded as if she'd just solved a math problem. "They're worried about bad publicity for the band. Do you think that guy James wants people to know Richie Taylor pays to have sex with a fifteen-year-old?"

"Don't talk like that!" Yolande said, her eyes lighting up with anger. "Richie really likes me."

"Gimme a break, Yo-yo!" Gabrielle threw her hands up into the air and sighed. "A lot of guys have been really liking you lately. Now Etienne's worried about business, and James is worried about Richie's wife and her dad and the band's reputation. Don't you think it's weird how, except for me, nobody's worried about you?"

Chapter 21

"Think there's hope?"

"There's always hope," Marcel said, running his fingers through Gabrielle's frizzy mop of hair. "If we layer the top near her face, we'll get rid of the bushiness." He sighed as if he knew it would be hard work.

"Go for it then," Yolande told him.

"I hate when people talk about me as if I'm not there," Gabrielle grumbled. But Marcel was already snipping and Yolande had picked up a *Vogue* magazine from the rack on the floor.

The haircut was Yolande's idea. She and Gabrielle had been reading a story about makeovers. "You could do more with yourself," Yolande had said. "Take advantage of your assets. Besides, it'll kill some time this weekend if we go to the spa." Focusing on somebody else distracted Yolande from her own problems — at least temporarily.

"Assets! What am I? An economics project?"

In the end, though, Gabrielle had agreed to let Marcel cut her hair and have one of the cosmeticians give her a makeup lesson.

"Hey, wasn't that you in *Meddler* magazine with Richie Taylor?" one of the assistants called out as she walked by with a pile of freshly folded towels.

Yolande lifted her head up from the magazine and looked the girl in the eye. "I don't know what you're talking about," she said with a smile.

Gabrielle leaned back into her chair. "No, no!" Marcel said in a voice that sounded like he was reprimanding a poodle for jumping up on the sofa. "Keep your head straight!"

Gabrielle straightened her head.

Marcel hummed as he worked. "Much better," he said as he snipped, adding to the mountain of dark curls on the floor.

"Phone call, Marcel!" the receptionist called, and Marcel put down his scissors and rushed to the front desk.

Yolande closed the magazine and examined Gabrielle. "Nice," Yolande said, "and it'll look even better after it's blow-dried."

Marcel waved two fingers at them from where he was standing. "I'll be two minutes!" They watched as he put his hand over the receiver. "It's my mom," he said, rolling his eyes.

Gabrielle nodded at Marcel, then turned back to Yolande. "I was thinking …" she began, lowering her voice.

"I hate when you do that."

"You hate when I think?"

"No, I hate when you begin a sentence with, 'I was thinking.' It means you're gearing up for one of your lessons."

"Fine then. I won't say anything." Gabrielle reached for a magazine, flicking it open.

"All right, what were you thinking?"

Gabrielle turned the magazine face down. "I was thinking you should stop."

"Stop what?"

"You know. The game." Gabrielle looked into Yolande's pale eyes.

"I can't just stop."

"Of course you can."

"I can't."

"Why not?"

Marcel was on his way back to the chair. "It's more complicated than you think," Yolande whispered. She meant the video, of course. Just thinking about it and about Etienne's threat to send it to her mom and her friends at the meditation centre made Yolande cringe. Sure, she was ashamed of the things she'd been caught doing on video, but she was even more ashamed that she'd let Etienne use her. And now she was way too ashamed to tell Gabs the whole truth.

Marcel opened his drawer and took out his blow-dryer. "I can do it curly or straight."

"Curly's fine," Gabrielle said.

"Straight," Yolande said.

Marcel opened his arms and lifted his palms into the air. "Look, I just got off the phone with my eighty-two-year-old mother; make things easy for me, okay?"

"Straight." Yolande said again. This time, Gabrielle didn't object.

"You look like a different person," Yolande said when Gabrielle's hair was dry.

"Straight hair gives her a more sophisticated look," Marcel said. "You know, honey," he told Gabrielle as he misted her hair with spray, "you might buy the Double Trouble leave-in conditioner I just used on you. It's super for controlling frizz."

"Double Trouble?" Gabrielle said. "Cool name."

"It's what happens when Gabs and I get together," Yolande told Marcel.

"I can see it," he said.

Next stop was a stool in the front window where Chantal, the cosmetician, worked. "I can tell you like a natural look," Chantal said when Gabrielle sat down. "A bit of pale, pink eyeshadow will set off your eyes."

"Don't put on too much," Gabrielle said, trying not to move.

Yolande sighed.

"Voilà," Chantal announced when she was finished, stepping away from the mirror to let Gabrielle see the results.

"Who're you?" Gabrielle asked her reflection.

Yolande whistled. "You look amazing."

"I do?"

Just then, the front door to the salon flew open and a blonde-haired woman rushed over to Chantal. "You have to do my makeup. Etienne and I are —"

It was Hélène. She stopped herself in mid-sentence when she saw Yolande. "What are you doing here?" she asked. "He told me he was sending you out of t —"

Hélène stopped herself again.

"What're you talking about?" Yolande asked. Her voice sounded like a kettle about to boil over. "He's not sending me anywhere!"

Hélène's pale skin turned even paler. "I … ah … must've made a mistake." Then she turned back to Chantal. "Do you think you can squeeze me in for a touch-up?"

Gabrielle tapped Yolande's shoulder. "Let's get out of here;" she whispered. "Now."

As they walked to the cash, they heard Hélène's voice over the whir of blow-dryers. "Who's that with her?" Hélène was asking. "She's a real looker."

Chapter 22

"He'd never send me away! Never!" Yolande chewed on the inside of her lip so hard she tasted blood.

She'd been trying not to let herself think that maybe Etienne really did want to get rid of her. But no matter how hard Yolande tried to block them out, anxious thoughts kept forcing their way in, like robbers with black stockings over their faces.

Maybe he thought she was used up, like that hooker on St-Laurent Blvd. Maybe he wanted her out of the way so he could be with Hélène. But no, that couldn't be! He loved her too much. Yolande knew he did … Didn't he?

It was 7:45 a.m. and she and Gabrielle were on their way to camp, their backpacks slung over their shoulders. On another day, Yolande might have taken some comfort in her routine — waking up, smearing her arms with sunscreen, meeting up with Gabs — but today, she just couldn't. Nothing about her life felt normal.

Gabrielle's hair was still straight, but she was wearing her usual makeup — none. In a tall maple tree overhead, a woodpecker made a drumming sound.

Up ahead, at the other end of Hampton Avenue, they could see two redheads — one tall, the other much shorter. It had to be the twins. William turned around and waved.

"Come on." Gabrielle said, taking bigger steps and grabbing Yolande's elbow, "Let's catch up with them."

Yolande sped up for a bit, then slowed down again. Her feet felt heavy. She had to stop to catch her breath. "I didn't get enough sleep," she said.

They walked on in silence. Then Yolande stopped again and reached for Gabrielle's hand. "I don't want to leave town," Yolande whispered, as if she were afraid that by speaking any louder she might make it happen. "I know I'm always complaining about my mom and how she's obsessed with meditation and health food, but that doesn't mean I wanna leave."

For a moment, Yolande closed her eyes and her voice turned dreamy. "Sure, maybe one day Etienne and I'll go someplace else and start over. But Gabs," and now Yolande opened her eyes, "you don't think he'd make me leave town, do you?" The words sounded more like a plea than a question.

At first, Gabrielle didn't say a thing. "I know he loves you," she said at last, as if she had chosen her words carefully, "and it could be Hélène just wants to upset you. But she really might know something. Maybe Etienne's so worried about the publicity and the police that he needs to get you out of town."

Though the air was as steamy as a sauna, Yolande shivered when she heard the word "police."

"If they find out about us and about what he does, they'll send him to jail." Her voice cracked.

"You know, maybe he's not the best guy for you," Gabrielle said quietly.

"How could you say that?" Yolande felt her heart start to race. It was one thing for her to doubt Etienne, but she couldn't bear for Gabrielle to do it.

Gabrielle took a step back.

That only made Yolande angrier. "You're supposed to be my best friend!" She kicked a recycling box that had been left lying near the curb. "All you ever do is criticize me!"

"I'm not criticizing you." Gabrielle dropped her voice. An elderly man, drawn by Yolande's shouting, was peeping out from behind his curtains. "I'm criticizing Etienne."

"Well don't! Next thing you'll be telling me I should turn him into the police!"

"Maybe you should!"

"You don't know anything about being in love!" Yolande brought her face so close to Gabrielle's, she could feel her breathing. "You have no idea what it feels like — how you can't imagine ever being apart, how just thinking about losing him makes you feel like … like you'll burst with sorrow!"

"Maybe you're right. But I know one thing: when someone loves you, they're supposed to treat you with respect."

"What's with you two?" William's booming voice interrupted them. The twins had stopped to let the girls catch up with them. Now they were only a couple of houses away.

"If you don't hurry up, we'll be late for camp!" Nick added.

"We didn't ask you to wait for us!" Yolande shouted back at the twins.

"We're just being gallant!" William answered back, poking his brother in the stomach. "Right?"

"Ready for another day with the rug rats?" Nick asked when the girls had caught up. "Hey, Gabrielle, what did you do to your hair? It looks weird."

William elbowed his brother in the ribs. "I think it looks nice," William said, his face reddening, so that for a second, it was almost the colour of his hair.

"How was your weekend?" Nick asked.

"Quiet," Yolande said, dropping her eyes to the sidewalk.

"Fine," Gabrielle added in a flat voice.

"Are you two in a fight again or something?" Nick asked.

Yolande and Gabrielle looked at each other. Gabrielle shrugged.

"What is it about girls that you're always fighting with each other?" Nick asked.

"We weren't fighting. Just discussing," Gabrielle said.

"I don't know how girls do it — fight, make up, then fight some more. Just talking about it wipes me out," Nick said as the four of them walked up to the Y.

"Shut up, will you?" William told his brother.

"Thanks," Gabrielle said, looking at William.

"No problem. I'm the sensitive twin," William said, throwing his shoulders back.

"Listen, there's something we wanted to ask you two." Nick slowed down on the stairs outside the Y. "But only if you two are getting along."

"We're getting along," Yolande said in a tired voice. "So what do you want to ask us?"

"Our folks are out of town, and our uncle's staying with us. We just got our driver's licenses, and we can use our dad's car, and well, we were wondering if —" Nick began.

"You wanted to go to a movie with us some time?" William finished his brother's sentence.

The two boys moved to the side of the stairs so a man carrying a gym bag could get by.

"Like maybe this weekend," Nick added hopefully.

"No, thanks," Yolande said, reaching for the door handle.

"Sure," Gabrielle said at the same time. She glared at Yolande.

Yolande glared back. Her hand was still on the handle. "Maybe," she said at last.

Nick gave William a high-five. "Good work, bro!" he said as they entered the building, squeezing past the bulletin board in the narrow vestibule.

"We'll see you at lunch, then," William said. He nodded at the girls before he and Nick headed for the locker room.

"Why'd you get me into that?" Yolande asked Gabrielle.

"They're nice guys. Besides, it'll beat house arrest."

"Yolande, there's a message for you," the receptionist called from the front desk when she spotted the girls. "A fellow named Etienne. He wants you to phone him right away. Says it's urgent."

"Gabs, look after my campers till I get there, okay?" Yolande's voice sounded normal, but her hands were shaking.

* * *

"We all fall DOWN!" the children cried out as they played ring-around-the-rosie in the field outside the Y. The air smelled of freshly mown grass, and in the distance, white sheets billowed on a clothesline.

Yolande's campers were lying on the grass laughing when she joined them.

"Everything okay?" Gabrielle asked, mouthing the words.

Yolande gave Gabrielle a thumbs-up.

"Listen," Gabrielle said, leaping up from the grass and addressing the campers, "we're gonna let you race from here to the slides and back. Can you guys handle that?"

"I love races," a voice shouted.

"Okay, then," Gabrielle said, lining up the children in a neat row. "On your marks, get set, go!"

The campers took off, screaming. Gabrielle immediately turned to Yolande. "What'd he say?"

"He said he thinks we need some time together. Just the two of us. So he wants to take me to the country for a couple of days."

"Uh-oh!"

"Don't go overreacting, Gabs. I'm excited." Yolande's voice had turned dreamy again. "It'll be our first trip together. I think Etienne's right. We need a chance to get things back on track. I have to be ready first thing tomorrow. He wants me to call in sick for camp."

"Are you sure it's a good idea?"

"It's an amazing idea."

Just then, one of the campers collapsed on the grass in front of them. "Yes!" he shouted. "I won!"

Chapter 23

Yolande picked up the telephone after the first ring. She'd known it would be Etienne. "Hey Tiffany," he said in his velvety voice. "Me and you still on for tomorrow?"

"Everything's arranged. I'll be at my corner for seven-thirty." Yolande examined her reflection in the mirror. A ray of late afternoon sun lit up her hair, making her feel more hopeful than she'd felt in a long time. Maybe things could still turn out to be okay. "I can't wait for us to be together."

"Me, too, babe. Now, don't be getting upset, but this thing's come up."

Yolande felt her body tense up.

"I'm gonna have to meet up with you later in the afternoon tomorrow," Etienne continued. "But Tiffany, I'm dying to have you to myself for a couple of days … and nights."

Yolande took a deep breath. The ray of sun had disappeared. "You haven't told me where we're going," she whispered.

"It's a surprise."

"I love surprises." Yolande tried to sound happy.

* * *

Yolande lay on her bed, staring up at the ceiling. She had to phone Gabrielle, but she couldn't do it right away. She had to take a little time to regroup, to calm down first. If she didn't, Gabs would know something was wrong. She was smart about stuff like that. When Yolande did call, she felt she had her voice under control.

"Gabs, you've gotta do me a favour."

"What kind of favour?"

"Just say you'll do it."

"But —"

"No buts."

"Okay, then," Gabrielle didn't sound happy. "What is it?"

"If my mom calls your house, you've gotta say I'm staying with you. It'll just be for a couple of days. So Etienne and I can have our little getaway."

"Are you sure —"

"Yes, I'm sure. So say okay?"

"Okay."

Yolande hung up the phone quickly. She didn't want to give Gabs a chance to change her mind.

* * *

"Vitality Vitamins. Sheila Owen speaking."

For a second, Yolande felt confused. She could never quite get used to her mother's office voice.

"Hi, Mom. Sorry to bug you at work."

"Why, hello, dear. What a surprise. You hardly ever call me just like that."

"Well, actually, I wanted to run something by you."

"Okay, go ahead." Yolande tried to ignore the fact that her mother sounded disappointed.

"I was wondering if I could spend a couple of days over at Gabs's. Starting tomorrow after camp. She and Aggie are almost finished their collage and they wanted to know if I could help. It's a pretty cool project. Very creative," Yolande added.

"Well, you know me," her mom sounded happier. "I like the idea of you getting in touch with your creative side. It'll help keep you balanced." Yolande could hear her mother tapping her pencil in the background. "You won't be gallivanting around 'til all hours now, will you?"

"Of course not."

"All right then. Just promise you'll remember my rule: home before dark."

* * *

"This is Yolande Owen and I'm afraid I won't be able to make it to camp tomorrow. I've got a bad code," she croaked into the telephone, adding a sniffle for effect.

"Geez, there must be something going around," said the person working the night desk at the Y. "Three other counsellors have phoned to say they won't be in tomorrow either."

Chapter 24

Sheila Owen was sitting cross-legged on a pillow in her meditation room, chanting, *"Om shanti,"* which meant "peace." The sweet smell of sandalwood incense wafted through the air.

"Om shanti!" Yolande said as she walked by.

Yolande wasn't feeling very peaceful. She'd just taken a shower, but her body already felt clammy. All night, she'd had one bad dream after another. In one, Etienne had tried to throw her off a bridge. She remembered how she'd looked into his eyes, thinking that would make him stop, but it hadn't. When her alarm went off, she awoke with the same desperate feeling she'd had in the dream.

"Have the granola and yogurt I left on the table," Mrs. Owen said, without moving from her pillow. "I'd join you, but I need to go deeper into my meditative state."

"Go for it, Mom," Yolande said, pausing in front of the door to what had once been the den, but was now the meditation room. Her mother's eyes were closed and she was breathing deeply, oblivious to Yolande now.

Yolande wished things were different. If only this room was still a den and her dad was still alive. If he was, maybe her mom wouldn't have become so weird. And maybe her own life would not have turned into such a disaster.

* * *

Desmond nodded when he saw Yolande walking towards the cab. Yolande's palms were damp, so she wiped them on her shorts. "Beautiful day, huh?" she said, trying to sound happy. The mountain ash trees were blooming. Their clusters of bright orange berries meant summer was coming to an end.

Soon, they were on the Decarie Expressway, heading north. Yolande tried to let herself imagine the two days ahead. She saw herself and Etienne, lying on some sandy beach, taking out a pedal boat when they felt like getting some exercise. She pictured the cottage where they'd stay. Made of thick wood logs, it would have a wraparound porch, where they'd read in the afternoon. At night, when the stars came out, they'd go for dinner, then come back to their cottage and make love. But when Yolande imagined Etienne, his eyes were as cold as they'd been in her dream.

"Where are you taking me?" she asked Desmond.

"No place special."

Yolande shivered. "No place special?" she asked, hugging herself. "That can't be," she added in a small voice. "Etienne told me he was taking me somewhere romantic."

Desmond shrugged. Now Yolande noticed a map of Quebec on the passenger seat.

"Etienne's not coming, is he?"

Desmond's eyes avoided hers in the rear-view mirror. "That's right," he said quietly.

Yolande clutched the bottom of her seat. "I hate him!" she said, loud enough for Desmond to hear her. "I so hate him!" Then she started to sob, her shoulders shaking and the tears streaming down her cheeks. She hadn't cried like this in years. Not since her dad died and she'd rolled around on the floor in her room, wailing like an animal. Remembering that made her cry even harder.

Without turning around, Desmond handed her a box of Kleenex.

"You have to tell me where we're going," Yolande said, blowing her nose. She could hear the panic building in her own voice. She remembered the fairy tale of Hansel and Gretel. She was like Gretel now — lost and far from home — only she didn't have pebbles or bread crumbs to throw out the window in case she needed to find her way back.

"Lachute."

"Lachute?" Yolande laughed out loud. "You're kidding, right? Lachute's a little hick town in the

154

middle of nowhere. What in the world does he expect me to do there?" Her voice was growing shrill.

"He's got a friend there. They're in the same line of work."

"He wants me to work for one of his friends?" Yolande's fingers reached for the door handle. Not that there was anywhere to go. Not on the highway, with the car travelling 100 kilometres an hour.

"You got it," Desmond said.

"What if I don't want to?"

"You're gonna need cash. And flipping burgers won't pay for those fancy clothes and shoes you like."

Looking around her, Yolande understood now that she was trapped. How had she gotten herself into this mess? Of course, she knew the answer. It was all because she'd fallen for Etienne. Let herself love him. And believe he loved her. She took a deep breath. "What's he doing today that's so important anyway?" she asked.

"I dunno."

"I bet you do know."

Desmond sighed. "All he told me is he wants me to pick him up at some art supply store on Ste-Catherine Street at four."

"What does he want with art supplies?" Yolande slid her fingers along the door handle.

"Don't ask me." Desmond looked into the rear-view mirror. "And quit playing with the door."

* * *

Yolande sat slumped in the back seat, her eyes half-closed, her chest heaving as she tried not to start crying again. She'd never felt more tired and down in all her life. It was like she'd fallen to the bottom of some pit — a place where it was cold and grey and rocky — and she didn't have the strength to pick herself up. She'd ruined everything.

She knew she had to try and come up with a plan, but she couldn't think straight. Images kept colliding in her head like bumper cars at La Ronde. Scenes from Etienne's video. The curly grey hair on Richie's chest. Her mom meditating. Aggie's collage. The bleached-blonde hooker leaning into a car on St-Laurent Boulevard. Etienne trying to throw her off the bridge.

Desmond pulled up in front of a red brick building. The sign outside said Central Hotel. It was one of those places that might have been a decent place to stay fifty years ago. Yolande peered up at the broken panes of glass over the door. By the side of the door, on a cardboard sign, printed in bold letters were the words: "Chambres par heure. Rooms by the hour." Yolande shuddered.

It was 9 a.m. Her campers would be playing with the parachute.

Yolande wrung her hands together as she looked up the street. There was an ice cream parlour, a Chinese restaurant, and a bowling alley.

Desmond scooped up Yolande's backpack. "I'll

take you upstairs," he said, swinging open the wooden door to the hotel.

The place smelled of mould. There was one elevator, but it was stuck on the fifth floor. Desmond pointed to a narrow stairwell. "We'll use the stairs."

There was no place else to go. No exit.

Yolande trudged upstairs behind Desmond. When they reached the second floor, he led her toward a room at the end of a dimly lit corridor. Now the air smelled of ammonia and mothballs. "It's us," he said, tapping on the door.

"Do you have her?" a husky voice asked.

"Bonjour! Bonjour!" The man behind the door was bald and overweight and his forehead glistened with sweat. "You heading back to Montreal, or do you wanna spend a little time here?" he asked, winking at Desmond.

"I'm going straight back," Desmond said, nodding at Yolande as he headed back down the corridor. "Look after her, will you?"

"I was hoping you'd look after me," the man said, chuckling at his own joke as he pulled Yolande inside. The room had no windows. The only furniture was a long bureau, a straight-backed wooden chair and a bed with a thin mattress that curled up at one end. Behind the bed, was a tinted mirror with thin, black ripples that reminded Yolande of gashes. "I like to sample the merchandise!" the man said with a rough laugh.

Yolande turned to look out the door and down

the long hallway at Desmond, who was already at the stairwell. "Please!" she cried out.

But Desmond's attention was elsewhere. Someone was rushing upstairs, trying to take two steps at a time. Yolande could tell it was a girl — one who wasn't used to wearing heels.

Whoever it was, was breathing heavily when she reached the second-floor landing. She had dark hair, had way too much makeup, and her skirt was hiked up to her thighs. "I need to make some money," she announced. "They told me to come up here and ask for Alex." Her tone was clipped, businesslike.

The dark eyes gave her away. It was Gabrielle.

Chapter 25

Yolande was standing behind Alex, her back pinned to the wall, the colour drained from her face. In the corner of the hotel room, an old fan rattled as it shifted from side to side. "Get out!" she said, mouthing the words at Gabrielle.

Gabrielle ignored her. She tapped her toes on the worn carpet as she waited for Alex's answer.

For a few seconds, all Alex did was smile. "Two girls," he said at last, making a *v* with his fingers and waving them in the air. "One blonde, one brunette. Sounds like a party to me! Must be my lucky day!" Then he licked his lips and patted his bulging stomach as if he was about to have a fine meal.

"So, you need cash?" he asked Gabrielle, sizing her up as he spoke.

Yolande inched away from the wall, making her way toward Gabrielle.

"That's right." Gabrielle raised her chin and looked Alex straight in the eye.

Yolande would never have guessed Gabrielle was capable of lying. It was as if she was seeing another side of her best friend — a side she'd never have expected. And where in the world had Gabrielle got those red slingback shoes?

"How did you know to come to me?" Alex asked Gabrielle.

"That sign downstairs — rooms by the hour — well that was pretty obvious. The clerk told me you were the one to talk to."

"You live around here?" Alex asked Gabrielle. His upper lip was beaded with sweat.

"Not far."

Alex rubbed his palms together. "Okay," he said, his voice turning serious as he addressed both girls. "This is how things work. I supply the clients and the rooms, and I make sure nobody roughs you up. I'm also in charge of the cash. You get seventy-five bucks at the end of every workday. That's a minimum of three johns. Do we have ourselves a deal?"

"It's a deal," Gabrielle said.

"Ninety. For her, too." Yolande raised her eyes toward Gabrielle.

"Eighty-five," Alex said. "Not a penny more."

Yolande nodded.

"I know Blondie's name is Tiffany; what's yours?" he asked Gabrielle.

"Sasha," Gabrielle answered, without hesitating.

Alex clapped his hands. "All right then, Sasha. Tiffany and I are going to have ourselves a party. But before we get started, I wanna call one of my buddies. He's got a thing for brunettes. Especially young ones. Only he likes to ride bareback."

"Whatever. I don't ca—"

"Bareback means he won't use a condom," Yolande interrupted. "It's not a good idea. My boyfriend in Montreal always made sure —"

"Your boyfriend?" Alex slapped his knee as if he'd heard a good joke. When he laughed, he made a guffawing noise and the flabby skin around his belly jiggled. "Listen. You two are working for me now. Besides, a lot of johns like it better bareback. You said you need money, Sasha. There's an extra twenty-five in it for you if you do him without a condom."

"Okay," Gabrielle said.

Alex grinned.

Yolande shook her head.

"I'll go ahead and make that call," Alex said, punching a number into his cellphone as he headed toward the bathroom. They could hear him lift the toilet seat, unbuckle his belt, and unzip his pants.

Gabrielle tugged on Yolande's sleeve. "Come on! Let's get outta here!" she whispered without taking her eyes off the bathroom door, which Alex had left half-open.

"What about him?"

"Hey, Blondie!" Alex called out as he began to pee. "Why don't you make yourself comfortable?" They heard him fumble with his cellphone. "Salut, Pierre," he said a moment later. "C'est moi, Alex. I'm at the hotel and I've got someone here I think you'd like to meet. Brown hair, good looking …" he paused as if he were saving the best news for last, "and young." Then he dropped his voice so the girls couldn't hear the rest of the conversation.

"I've got an idea," Gabrielle whispered, eyeing the bureau on the side wall. "A way to keep him in there!" she told Yolande.

"Oh, what a beautiful morning! Oh, what a beautiful day!" Alex sang as he turned on the faucet.

"Hey, baby," Yolande called out so Alex would hear her over the sound of the running water, "why don't you take a shower? Nothing turns me on more than a guy who smells like soap."

Yolande and Gabrielle smiled at each other when they heard Alex slap his knee again. "Nothing turns me on more than a girl who's turned on. Hey, I've got a better idea — come on in here and have a shower with me! Tell Sasha she can go next door to wait for her john. Room two-oh-four."

Yolande giggled as loudly as she could. "I'll be right in," she called out. "Sasha, he wants you to go to room 204."

The bureau was heavier than it looked. They each took one end, hoisting it up an inch or two so Alex wouldn't hear them drag it across the room.

As the girls approached the crack in the bathroom door, they saw Alex's pants and shirt drop to the tile floor. There were dark sweat stains under the shirt's armpits. Yolande hoped she wouldn't see him naked.

Distracted by the thought of what Alex might

look like naked, Yolande lost her grip on the bureau. The corner she was holding slipped from her hands. She imagined the crashing sound it would make if it hit the wall — and how angry Alex would be when he discovered what they were up to.

But Gabrielle quickly seized one of the drawer handles and pulled back on it so the bureau fell softly down onto the carpet. One of her red sling backs slid from her foot. Instead of trying to get it back on, she kicked the other shoe off, too.

Suddenly, they heard the heavy thud of Alex's steps on the bathroom floor. He seemed to be coming closer. Yolande and Gabrielle froze, the bureau still between them. Had he heard them?

A moment later, they heard him step into the shower.

"Phew! That was a close c—" Yolande said.

Gabrielle raised her eyebrows, reminding Yolande it was better not to make any unnecessary noise.

They went back to work, lifting the bureau and carrying it across the room. The bathroom door was only about a foot away now. Yolande's biceps ached. They were nearly there.

A cloud of hot steam drifted out into the hotel room. "Hey, baby! I'm ready for you!" Alex called out.

"I'm almost undressed!" Yolande managed to call back.

"Oh, what a beautiful morning!" Alex sang from the shower.

When they finally dropped the bureau an inch from the bathroom door, Yolande and Gabrielle didn't stop to look at each other. There wasn't time.

Gabrielle reached for the doorknob, gritting her teeth as she shut the door. Any noise now would ruin their plan.

As quietly as they could, the girls positioned the bureau so it blocked the bathroom door.

"Let's go!" Gabrielle whispered, grabbing Yolande's hand.

As the girls made a run for it, the Do Not Disturb sign swung like a pendulum on the door handle.

"Take the stairs!" Gabrielle said as they raced down the corridor. Again, Yolande did as she was told.

The walls must have been paper thin, because when they were halfway down the corridor, they heard Alex bellow, "What the hell are you two bitches up to?" Then there was a crashing sound. Alex must have been pounding on the bathroom door.

Yolande and Gabrielle rushed down the stairs.

They were breathing so heavily they couldn't speak. But when Gabrielle saw Yolande press her palm on the door that led from the stairwell into the lobby, her eyes lit up.

"Not that door!" she said, panting as she tried to catch her breath. "This way! The twins are waiting out back!"

Chapter 26

"The twins? What are they —" Yolande asked as they opened the door and stepped out into the hotel parking lot.

Gabrielle pushed Yolande into the twins' car. "Move it, Yo-yo!"

Yolande wiped her forehead as she slid into the back seat.

"Okay, drive!" Gabrielle shouted, slamming the car door behind her. William, who was at the wheel, squealed out of the narrow lane at the back of the hotel. "Do you have to make so much noise?" Gabrielle asked.

"Don't bug him," Nick said. "He's not accustomed to driving getaway vehicles."

Yolande opened her arms and hugged Gabrielle. For a moment, they just clung to each other. Both of them were shaking. As Yolande held Gabrielle, she realized how strong and wiry her friend was. "I can't believe you did that," she said.

Gabrielle smiled at Yolande. "We did it."

"I could never have gotten out of there without you."

"Remember that next time you're dumping on me for being a lousy friend." Gabrielle attached her seat belt. "Hey," she said, looking over at Yolande, "Buckle up."

"You left your shoes upstairs," Yolande said.

"Oh, well," Gabrielle said, looking down at her bare feet. "They weren't exactly my style."

When William turned onto Rue Principale, Gabrielle craned her neck to look behind her. Except for a milk truck, there was no traffic.

"How'd she convince you two to drive all the way out here?" Yolande asked.

"That Gabrielle can be pretty convincing," William said without taking his eyes off the road.

"Yeah, she phoned us last night. I figured it was about the movie. But no such luck," Nick added.

"She told us she needed some wheels. And you know us — always ready to help our fellow counsellors."

"Especially if it means missing arts and crafts," Nick said.

They were approaching the highway. "Where to now?" William asked.

"Back to Montreal. St-Denis Street. We're going to find Yolande's boyfriend."

Yolande's eyes had begun to glisten with tears. "I don't want to see him again! Ever!"

"You have to," Gabrielle insisted. "How else

166

are you going to get him to leave you alone?"

"He'll never leave me alone," Yolande whispered. They'd managed to escape Alex and his seedy hotel, but Yolande knew escaping Etienne wouldn't be quite so easy. Again, she remembered how cold his eyes had been in her dream.

"Oh, yes he will," Gabrielle said.

"Don't try to talk me into turning him in. I couldn't do it. I just couldn't."

Nick turned to look at the girls. "If you want to know my opinion, he doesn't sound like a very nice guy."

"You told them everything?" Yolande asked. Now the tears began to spill down her cheeks. She wiped them away with the back of her hand.

"I had to."

"I feel so stupid," Yolande said, sniffling. "Now everyone is going to know."

"The main thing is you're safe." Gabrielle patted Yolande's knee.

"You don't have to worry about us. We're not going to tell anyone about — well, you know …" William said.

Nick squirmed in his seat. "I mean, it's not like we're gonna go around telling people, 'This girl we know from camp's a hook —"

William leaned over and elbowed Nick. "Sometimes my brother can be a real asshole," he said.

"Ouch," Nick said, rubbing his forearm. "That hurt."

"So why don't you go the police?" William

asked after they'd driven a little further.

When Yolande answered, her voice was very low. "Like I said before, I just couldn't. I know you'll think I'm crazy, but I feel like a part of me'll always love Etienne. No matter what. Besides, even if I didn't feel that way, I couldn't stand having the police asking me questions. They'd think I really was a — a —" Yolande took a deep breath, "a — whore."

After that, the car was silent. They were all thinking about what Yolande had said.

It was William who finally broke the silence. "Which block on St-Denis Street are we going to?" he asked.

Yolande eyed the clock on the dashboard. It was 2:05 p.m. If the traffic wasn't heavy, they'd be back in Montreal before four. "He won't be there."

"Where's he going to be?" Gabrielle said

"At the art supply store on Ste-Catherine Street."

"What in the world does he want with art supplies?" Gabrielle asked.

*   *   *

A girl with long hair the colour of Yolande's was standing in the store window. She couldn't have been much older than Aggie. She was pretending to examine easels, but every few seconds she'd lift her head to peer out at the street. You could tell she was waiting for someone.

"I'll go with you," Gabrielle said as William scanned the street for parking.

"No," Yolande said. "I got myself into this and it's up to me to get myself out. Look, there's a parking spot. You guys wait here. I'll wave if I need help."

"Are you sure you don't want us to go in with you? For moral support?" William asked.

"I'm sure." Yolande let herself out of the car.

Gabrielle moaned as she watched Yolande head for the store. "It's like I'm watching a horror movie. Only it's real."

"What are you talking about?" Nick asked.

Gabrielle lifted her chin in the direction of a young black man sauntering up the street. His head was shaven. "Meet Etienne."

* * *

"What the hell are you doin' here?" Etienne's voice didn't sound anything like liquid honey. He didn't give Yolande a chance to answer. Instead, he kept firing questions at her. "Why aren't you in Lachute? Where's Desmond? What the hell's going on?" He reached into his pocket for his cellphone. "Wait'll I talk to that screw-up!" he muttered.

"I came t-t-to tell you to leave me alone." Yolande stammered as she looked into the familiar brown eyes. The eyes she loved. Or used to love. It was all so confusing.

Etienne hit the speed-dial on his phone. Yolande could hear the phone ring on the other end. "Answer, you idiot!" Etienne muttered. When no one picked up, he folded the phone in two and shoved it back into his pocket.

Yolande straightened her spine and willed herself to be strong, not to go falling for him all over again. To resist him. "We have to talk," she said.

Etienne laughed. The old laugh, only there was something rough sounding about it. "Get outta my way," he said, pushing open the door to the store.

Yolande didn't move. "I mean it," she said. The words came more easily now. But she shuddered when she realized Etienne's eyes were just as cold as they'd been in her dream. "I want you to leave me alone."

"I'm not done with you yet."

They were only an inch or two apart and with Etienne looking at her, Yolande felt like she might lose her balance. He wasn't done with her. Did that mean he thought they could still be together? Part of her still wished there was some way of going back to how they used to be.

Yolande blinked. Be strong, she reminded herself as she opened her eyes. Remember how he sent you to Lachute and how he expected you to work for that disgusting Alex.

"If you don't leave me alone, I'm gonna tell the … the police about you. And about your girls." It was hard to say the words, but there, she'd done it.

There was a tapping sound. It was the girl in the

window. Now she was waving at Etienne, unaware, it seemed, that he and Yolande were having an argument.

"I could hurt you," Etienne said, smiling as he turned to wave back at the girl. "Or your friends."

Yolande shivered as she looked up the street to where the twins' car was parked.

That made Etienne smile again. He grabbed Yolande's hand. For a second, she thought he was going to squeeze it, but instead, he twisted her wrist.

"Ow!" Yolande cried out. She pulled her hand away. Then she looked at him, peered at him really, as if she'd never seen him before. The weird thing was, he looked the same. But Yolande knew this wasn't the old Etienne — the one she'd fallen in love with — the one who'd made her feel important and loved.

Maybe that Etienne had never existed. Maybe she'd imagined him all along. That thought hurt even more than her wrist, which had begun to throb. "How could you?" she asked. She wasn't just talking about her wrist.

"Easily." Etienne looked down at Yolande's wrist. "And you'll cooperate unless you want more of that." His eyes were as cold as steel. "Now go home. Don't even think of leaving your house 'til you hear from me. In the meantime, I've got business to take care of."

Yolande rubbed her wrist with her other hand. He didn't love her. He *never had*. She watched as he turned his back on her and walked into the store. As if she had meant nothing to him. That was exactly it. She had meant nothing to him. She was just a commodity to be bought and sold — or rented out by the hour. The worst part was that she had let him do it.

For a moment, Yolande couldn't speak. It was as if the words in her head were trapped somewhere between her brain and her throat. But she knew she had to speak up. If not for herself, then for that girl in the window — and all the other girls who might meet Etienne or someone like him. Unless she did something about it.

"Wait!" Yolande called out. "You know that video? The one of me and you doing it? The one you said you had a copy of — stashed away for safekeeping?"

Etienne spun around. His eyes looked like they'd caught fire. "What about it?"

"You gave me the idea. Only I didn't make a video. I wrote out five reports — they're sort of like term papers — and I left them with five different people. For safekeeping. I included everything I know about you: your friends, the places where you hang out, your address, and the work you do. The pimping."

Etienne stared hard at Yolande. "I don't believe you."

"You'd better believe me." Even Yolande was surprised by how determined she sounded. "If anything bad happens to me, or to anyone I know, those reports are going to *Meddler* magazine. And to the police. In fact, if I were you, I'd give up the game. Just in case I decide to send those reports anyway."

Yolande took a deep breath. She'd said it all. For some reason, the words "*Om shanti*" popped into her head. She needed all this to be over. She needed peace.

Etienne shifted from one foot to the other as he looked at Yolande. She wouldn't let herself turn away. He had to know she was serious — that she really would turn him in to the police if she had to.

"All right," Etienne said, with a small nod. "I'll let you be. Just so you know, I was planning to come and meet you in Lachute so we could have some time together. Just us."

Yolande sucked in her breath. The hardest part wasn't letting go of Etienne. The hardest part was letting go of the Etienne she'd imagined him to be. He had never planned to meet her in Lachute. "No you weren't." Her voice was calm. "You'd better leave her alone, too," Yolande added, glancing up at the store window.

Etienne obviously hadn't expected her to guess why he was at the art supply store. He slumped a little. Then he nodded.

Yolande watched Etienne walk down Ste-Catherine St., his hands buried in his pockets. She knew she should hate him, but she didn't. She looked into the store window. The girl was gone.

Yolande gazed at her own reflection. How could

she have let him con her? When she looked at herself, she didn't see blue eyes or blonde hair or long legs or an expensive T-shirt; she saw something else, someone new. It wasn't the girl she'd been before she'd met Etienne. That girl was gone forever. What she saw was a girl who'd been confused, who'd made mistakes, but who was trying to begin to set things right.

Someone rushed out onto the sidewalk. It was the blonde girl from inside the store and she was stomping her foot. "How come you made him leave?" she demanded. "I met him here last week and he's the coolest guy. He said he'd take me out for coffee."

Yolande smiled at the girl. "You're too young for coffee," she said.

As Yolande walked back to the twins' car, she took a last look up Ste-Catherine Street. Etienne was at the intersection. In the distance, he looked small. Almost harmless.

Chapter 27

When the phone rang, Mrs. Owen didn't get up from the kitchen table where she was hunched over a sheet of bristol board.

"I'll get it!" Yolande reached for the phone. "It's Judith from the meditation centre. She wants to know if you're coming to *satsang* tomorrow."

"Tell her I'll phone her later, will you, honey?"

When Mrs. Owen had learned the truth about Yolande, she'd been determined to go to the police and press charges against Etienne. But Yolande had managed to talk her out of it.

"I'm not ready," Yolande had told her, "Not yet, anyway. You can't make me do something like that if I'm not ready."

In the end, Mrs. Owen had agreed not to put more pressure on Yolande. For now, they had decided to focus on strengthening their own relationship — spending more time together and beginning to talk about some of the things they'd both been avoiding for a long time. Yolande was beginning to feel happier, and she'd noticed her mom seemed happier, too. It was like she was grateful just to be let in, to be part of Yolande's life again.

"I never thought I'd be the type to enjoy working on a collage," Mrs. Owen said when Yolande sat back down. Yolande was wearing a faded pair of low-rise jeans and at the small of her back you could see the tops of the letters E.G., looking like a jagged mountaintop.

She hadn't gotten around to going back to Rush, though she'd decided she didn't want Etienne's initials turned into a flower or a bird. "I want a dragon," she'd told Gabrielle. "Something strong and fiery."

Mrs. Owen passed Yolande a small pile of photographs.

"Gabrielle says doing collage is a way of making sense of all the pieces in your life," Yolande said as she examined the pictures. "Hey, Mom, is this you in the halter top?"

Mrs. Owen looked at the photograph and sighed. "I don't know how my mother ever let me out of the house wearing that thing. We don't have to use it, do we?"

"Oh, yes we do!" Yolande took the photograph from her mother.

Mrs. Owen cleared her throat. "You know, I haven't told you this, but I wasn't the easiest teenager myself."

"I had a feeling. So … are you ever going to tell me about it?"

Mrs. Owen studied the piece of bristol board as if it were a map. "Maybe one day." There was a long pause. "Do you still think about him and well … everything that happened?" Mrs. Owen asked.

Yolande turned away. "Uh-huh," she said. "Sometimes."

"It gets easier."

Yolande looked back at her mother. "It does?"

"Uh-huh. It's hard to explain," Mrs. Owen said. "The bad memories never disappear completely. They just become part of you. Part of your story. And then somehow, you keep going."

Yolande rested her chin on one hand and nodded. She studied the photo of her mom. Picking the scissors up from the table, she considered cutting out just the face and torso. Then she put the scissors down. The sky in the background of the photo was bright blue. It would suit the collage.

"I think I'm gonna be okay," Yolande said softly.

Mrs. Owen smiled. For a second, Yolande thought she was about to mention lecithin or *chi* energy, but she didn't.

"You know, Mom, it's the other girls I'm worried about. The ones who are going to fall for guys like Etienne and then get tangled up in … you know … the game. I'm still not ready to press charges against him — not for now, at least — but I think about those other girls a lot."

Now Mrs. Owen nodded. "I think about them, too. But it occurred to me that maybe one day — when you're ready — you might be able to help those girls."

"You mean by going to the police?"

"There's that, of course. But there's something else, too — something that might make a difference to those girls."

Yolande looked up at her mother. "What's the something else?"

"Telling them your story."

Their eyes met. "Maybe one day," Yolande said.